I AM DEATH

I AM

DEATH

TWO NOVELLAS BY GARY AMDAHL

MILKWEED EDITIONS

Published 2008 by Milkweed Editions
Printed in Canada
Cover design by Christian Fünfhausen
Author photo by Erin Schneider
Interior design by Connie Kuhnz, BookMobile Design and Publishing Services, Minneapolis, Minnesota.
The text of this book is set in Slimbach.
08 09 10 11 12   5 4 3 2 1
First Edition

Milkweed Editions, a nonprofit publisher, gratefully acknowledges sustaining support from Anonymous; Emilie and Henry Buchwald; the Bush Foundation; the Patrick and Aimee Butler Family Foundation; CarVal Investors; the Dougherty Family Foundation; the Ecolab Foundation; the General Mills Foundation; the Claire Giannini Fund; John and Joanne Gordon; William and Jeanne Grandy; the Jerome Foundation; Dorothy Kaplan Light and Ernest Light; Constance B. Kunin; Marshall BankFirst Corp.; Sanders and Tasha Marvin; the May Department Stores Company Foundation; the McKnight Foundation; a grant from the Minnesota State Arts Board, through an appropriation by the Minnesota State Legislature, a grant from the National Endowment for the Arts, and private funders; an award from the National Endowment for the Arts, which believes that a great nation deserves great art; the Navarre Corporation; Debbie Reynolds; the Starbucks Foundation; the St. Paul Travelers Foundation; Ellen and Sheldon Sturgis; the Target Foundation; the Gertrude Sexton Thompson Charitable Trust (George R. A. Johnson, Trustee); the James R. Thorpe Foundation; the Toro Foundation; Moira and John Turner; United Parcel Service; Joanne and Phil Von Blon; Kathleen and Bill Wanner; Serene and Christopher Warren; the W. M. Foundation; and the Xcel Energy Foundation.

Library of Congress Cataloging-in-Publication Data

Amdahl, Gary, 1956–
    I am death : two novellas / by Gary Amdahl. — 1st ed.
        p.   cm.
    ISBN 978-1-57131-071-2 (pbk. : alk. paper)
    I. Title.
    PS3601.M38I3 2008
    813'.6—dc22

                                2008000365

This book is printed on acid-free paper.

MINNESOTA
STATE ARTS BOARD

NATIONAL
ENDOWMENT
FOR THE ARTS

For Leslie, again and always

I AM DEATH
TWO NOVELLAS

I AM DEATH

"Had he heard these stories from someone else, or
had he made them up himself in the remote past,
and afterwards, as his memory grew weaker, mixed
up his experiences with his imaginations and became unable to distinguish one from the other?
Anything is possible, but it is strange that on this
occasion and for the rest of the journey, whenever
he happened to tell a story, he gave unmistakable
preference to fiction."

Anton Chekhov, *The Steppe*

"The violation of a confidence is also this: not just
being indiscreet and thereby causing harm or ruin,
not just resorting to that illicit weapon when the
wind changes and the tide turns on the person who
did the telling and the revealing—and who now
regrets having done so and denies it and grows confused and sombre, wishing he could wipe the slate
clean, and who now says nothing—it is also pro-
fiting from the knowledge obtained through another's weakness or carelessness or generosity, and not
respecting or remembering the route by which we
came to know information that we are now mani-
pulating or twisting."

Javier Marías, *Your Face Tomorrow:*
Fever and Spear

"No themes are so human as those that reflect for us, out of the confusion of life, the close connexion of bliss and bale, of the things that help with the things that hurt, so dangling before us forever that bright hard medal, of so strange an alloy, one face of which is somebody's right and ease and the other somebody's pain and wrong."

Henry James, Preface to *What Maisie Knew*

I Am Death, or, Bartleby the Mobster
(A Story of Chicago)

[1]

DEATH BEGINS THE STORY. I talk for a while, then fall silent. That's life: from "death" to "death," the story pops into being, miraculously, then you forget about it. In the middle years, you do what you can, you overdrive your headlights, you speed weightlessly down a road in thick fog, the road becomes a bridge, the bridge rises higher and higher, becomes narrower and narrower, then, achingly, stops in midair, pieces of it jutting blackly and dangling in the wind. The people you love most in your life are staring at you with hatred, you're shrieking at them and crying your eyes out, you can't stop, it almost feels good to sob this way. Abraham kills Isaac.

I am a journalist. This is a story I am compelled to report. I don't want to, I'm tired of banging my head against the wall, no one I know is the least bit interested in *cause* anymore, *effect* is everything. Trace an effect back to the least outbuilding of corporate culture and you're finished. This story, too, I admit, is infatuated with effect, its principals fairly staggered with consequence, but the cause is there, swinging back and forth like a hypnotist's watch: I can't make out the time and I'm getting sleepy.

I graduated from high school the year Nixon resigned, and was caught up in the rigor and stink of muckraking, the virtuous thrills of exposing the lies of power celebrities. My first job was at the *Cambridge Chronicle*, part-time reporting work supplemented by the writing of events publicity at MIT, where I buddied up to Noam Chomsky. Then I became the editor of *The Circle*, the newspaper of the Boston Indian Council, where I buddied up to Louise Erdrich. I married a dancer,

Dorothy Roff Gorton, of the Connecticut Roff Gortons—if you follow dance you maybe saw her in Martha Clarke's *The Garden of Earthly Delights*. We moved to Chicago—after Dorothy got hit by a cab, a glancing blow, but it ended her career—where I worked at the City News Bureau. A year later, I was Midwest Correspondent for *Life*. An indeterminate number of years went by, I quit *Life*, Dorothy left me. Now I am freelancing, writing things like advertising supplements for the Schaumburg Chamber of Commerce, a series of pieces on the history of Schaumburg, all titled "Schaumburg!"

I was once more than receptive to the idea that my failure to become the kind of reporter I thought I'd become could be attributed to the demise of the free press, but I see it quite differently now.

TRANSCRIPT OF TELEPHONE CONVERSATION WITH DONALD KING, CEO, PIZZA KING, INC., DECEMBER 3RD, 1988

ME: "A fatality or two"? I wonder if that isn't similar to what you were saying earlier, umm, I mean that you can *accept* maybe "a fatality or two" *because of* the size of the business, and since fatalities are, as you say, inevitable, does that almost make it okay?

KING: I suppose if—Of course you can never do enough, isn't that right? I mean, I'm not sure what you're implying here! Let me just say that to prevent fatalities or accidents, if uh, if uh, well, if the world is going to judge me, we're doing a damn good job. *Compared to the rest of the world.* If I'm going to judge myself, I may not be so happy. I don't know how many years now we've been working with the National Safety Council—and it's very difficult you see when you've got stores scattered all over—

ME: Well that's yes that's just what I'm saying, the bigness—

KING: —and yes, the bigness and the part-time drivers and the, the college students who—the turnover you see is horrendous! But compared to the rest of the industry, Mr. umm, Mr.—

ME: Jack.

KING: Mr. Jack, compared to—

ME: Just Jack, first name.

KING: Compared to Jack, I mean, compared, Jack, to the rest of the industry, we do twice as well, three times as well. Compared to what I'd like to do—

ME: I guess I'm wondering, given the fatalities, the inevitable as you say, given that people are dying, I'm wondering if you haven't thought about giving up the business or what I mean is that part of the business that depends on the thirty-minute delivery policy, which—

KING: No, no, no, what? No, look, look, whenever the pizza is twenty-five minutes old, and that's just about the minimum from order to out-the-door, we mark it late, you see. *It's always late*, in effect, so there's no reason for the driver to hustle it to the customer and in so doing risk his, risk his—it *makes no difference*, you see, *to the driver*. We mark it late and subtract three dollars automatically and maybe the customer gives the guy a bigger tip because of it. Do you understand what I'm . . . ?

ME: Well, I'm not sure, that's why I'm asking—

KING: It almost sounds a little, you know, accusatory. That I'm doing something that uh, that's causing unnecessary deaths and injuries and what have you and I'm not doing anything about it.

ME: I apologize if I sound accusatory. It's just that when we talked last, we did spend some time on philosophical issues, about your religion and your convictions and your, specifically, your respect for life, and these are things I figure you must be thinking about as you conduct your business, and I don't mean to sound accusatory but maybe I am a little bit. I've been urged on by my editors, who have asked me to definitely address this issue, since it's something that's gotten so much attention lately.

KING: Well certainly and I yes—

ME: It's not going to dominate the interview by any means.

KING: I think it would be unfair if it did. It comes out like I do right to life on the one hand and—and—and—kill innocent people on the—The thirty-minute policy is part of an advertising strategy, that's all. The drivers, you see—

ME: So you're, excuse me, you're saying, if I can clarify this, the drivers should not have to die in the service of an advertising campaign, am I, is that what you're, is that fair? A promise you never intended to keep?

KING: No, no, no.

ME: But they are dying and it's basically, correct me if I'm wrong about this, they're dying because they don't understand they don't have to? It's just advertising, but they think it's for real? Maybe they feel duty-bound, they're trying to do right by the company, *your* company, *their* company, to honor what they perceive to be something more important than an advertising gimmick and that is, or would be, I'm suggesting, the honor or integrity of the commitment the company has made, to the public, to the consumer.

KING: That is not at all how it is, that is so wrong, that's just insulting!

ME: No reason for you to be upset. Frankly, you want to talk about advertising, there are ad dollars that make this rag I'm working for possible, and they don't want to see you and people like you made controversial. My editors know this and actually haven't urged me on at all. I just wanted to know, for myself, as a citizen. Thanks for your time. Thanks very much. Good-bye.

END OF TRANSCRIPT

That was the last work that I would characterize as hard-hitting. A list of projects I was working on just before I got the call leading to the present story: walking the beat with two cops from Broadway to Marine on Wilson, and along Broadway from Roscoe to Diversey; listening to conversations in a barbershop in Mundelein, where "economic growth" was being viewed askance ("We're going to become another Schaumburg if we don't watch out!" one old customer shouted at me); a brief history of computers, featuring the heroic salvaging of the legendary 1945 Whirlwind; and a piece on "toner phoners" and "paper pirates," who sell copy machine toner and inferior grades of paper at exorbitant prices over the phone to gullible or careless office managers. A piece on wellness was killed the very day mob lawyer George Swanson called me.

"It's too negative."

"All I did was quote the experts."

"You should have talked to different experts, Jack. Wellness is all about being positive, get it?"

Yes, I see it quite differently now. I'm just one of those arrows Scott Fitzgerald talked about, shot from obscurity to obscurity. I have come to tell this story not because I am a great man, a hero, but because its characters came to me like characters in a fairy tale and promised to set me free, to keep the arrow magically aloft in a blaze of light, if I in turn would promise to help the world understand them, the Chicago hoodlum who did a little Cuba, did a little Hoffa, a little Vegas, who wandered from room of money to room of guns to room of lawyers, gesturing casually but precisely with his long, fine, cold hands and black, glassy eyes for the slaughter of one, ten, a hundred men—and his adviser, who let his strange and powerful mind become sodden with oily greed, chug to a stop, and catch fire. If we are villains, the mouthpiece insisted, we are villains with a difference!

But the man who must beg to have his story told knows in his heart it's too late. He suspects something has gone wrong. And as the arrow descends into the gloom and murk, he grows deaf and dumb.

[2]

I ALSO WROTE A MONTHLY COLUMN for one of those news and arts weeklies: *The Meaning of Life.* (The reader may recall a while back a year in which the American people were said to be terribly concerned about the meaning of life. In a couple of polls it beat out a balanced budget and health care.) All I had to do was ask the people I met in the course of a day what they thought the meaning of life was, record their answers on tape, and take their pictures. For instance: when walking the beat with a couple of cops on Broadway, we saw to the needs of some gentlemen drinking from paper bags behind a pharmacy. I asked one who appeared to be the spokesperson what he thought the meaning of life was, and he didn't hesitate a second. "This officer could have put us in the wagon and took us downtown for detox. Thank you," he said, grinning toothlessly for my camera, "for not doing it!" The toner-phoner said, "Being the best at what you do and never looking back. This is a nation of salesmen, right? Dinner and movie absolutely. A legacy for your children's children? I don't think so. It's too intangible."

The last column I put together, the one that prompted George Swanson to contact me on behalf of his client Frank Fini (they read it religiously, he told me, together, from beginning to end), was a special triple-length feature that came out of a Saturday night at the Cook County morgue. I spoke to several people there: Jude Hawkins, a round, unshaven, pasty-faced fellow who described himself—while he was tapping furiously on a computer keyboard with cartoons about death and injunctions about system use taped all over it, trying to requisition himself a new corpse-measuring stick—as a conservative Christian and lover of musical comedy; Helen Antrobus, a data entry clerk who didn't understand the question; Ann Boehm, a biker chick sporting a swastika tattoo on her forearm; and Henrique Friend. This last name may ring a bell with you, even if you reside outside Chicagoland. Ricky was nineteen and delivered bodies to the morgue, driving a gray government van to and from all the many places in the metropolitan area where people had died, downtown to the cooler. He looked strikingly like the Lord Byron of the Thomas Phillips oil in the National Portrait Gallery in London (the pencil-thin mustache, the gaudy silk wound around his head, the romantic posture), and had tried, depressed uncontrollably by the work he did, not three months earlier, to kill himself.

I AM DEATH

EXCERPT FROM TRANSCRIPT OF CONVERSATION WITH HEN-
RIQUE FRIEND, COOK COUNTY MORGUE, FEBRUARY 15TH, 1989

RICKY: Working here, man, *bueno*, it's hard, it's strange, you always feel like I'm late, I missed it, there's nothing you can do. You figure out how to be here and you get used to it.

END OF EXCERPT

Confessing easily to me that the place frightened him, or saddened him—he wasn't sure and decided to let it go—and assuring me that I would feel the same way, Ricky showed me the cooler. He seemed apprehensive but eager. When we got inside, he stood by the big, heavy, cold door, his arms wrapped around himself the way a modern dancer might do it, on his face a look that almost passed for chilly glee, as if he were waiting on a sidewalk for the other carolers to arrive. He looked lost. Not despairing, necessarily, but as if uncertain where next to turn, what next to say, and seeing the possibilities for the next step, the next word, dwindle and disappear altogether. I too began to feel confused. I saw my breath condense and hang in the air, as if I were slowing down and stopping. As if I might see, in the frozen stillness, clearly, for an instant, the one thing I needed to see, to either go on living, or not.

The cooler was as big as a gymnasium, cold and silent, with two hundred and fifty bodies on display, as if in a museum, or the backstage workshop of a museum, figures in various states of disrepair and corruption. Here was the man whose co-worker had missed a stud and fired a nail from an automatic nailer through a piece of wallboard into his friend's heart. Here was the infant who had fallen into a bucket of mop water and drowned. Here was the old man who had starved to death and the old woman who'd fallen down a flight of stairs, her skin a taut, dry bag punctured here and there with broken pieces. Here was a female who'd lain for many years in a shallow grave. Here was a man whose head had been severed in a car accident. Here were two lovers who'd fallen asleep in the back seat while carbon monoxide fumes assailed them like guilt-laden dreams. Here was an entire family as if in a Republican Party fund-raising exhibit, unblemished but unmoving. Here were assorted gang members, frayed holes in flannel shirts matching deep black holes in their flesh, at the bottoms of which resided slugs. Here was someone who appeared, medievally, to have been drawn and quartered, limbs stacked neatly by his side on the stainless steel tray. And here was the young mother, pregnant again, unrecognizable to the young father in her shrunken state, her skin crisp and black like obsidian but preserving in its strange shape the image of her final thought, the molten tongue in the gaping crucible of the mouth saying the word, the vacant orbits of the eyes retaining still something of the blinding light of that word, the charred and splintered bones of her arms held out imploringly or perhaps in invitation, asking for and promising great love, the greatest love, free and eternal, without condition, but, finally, without foundation.

I said to Ricky, "It's too much," to which he replied, "Either that or not enough."

[3]

EXCERPT FROM TRANSCRIPT OF CONVERSATION WITH HENRIQUE FRIEND, COOK COUNTY MORGUE, FEBRUARY 15TH, 1989

RICKY: To my purpose in living I don't know, I got so many friends and so many relatives but sometimes I feel alone and then I think about trying to take my life away but then I think about well, why should I do it? To me the purpose of living because first of all, if you are born there's two things that you should have to choose: either you are going to be a good person or you are going to be a bad person. And if you are going to be that person, everybody's going to have to die, no matter what, anyway. Even animals die. Plants

die, water dries up, planes fall out of the—I mean, the world is just
fucked up. The way I see it, it's just not right.

END OF EXCERPT

George Swanson read this back to me over the phone, read it
like a bad actor, even trying a Hispanic street accent here and there.
He thought it was the most interesting thing he'd read in a newspaper in years, it really got to the heart of something, especially with
the uncorrected grammar, and would I be able to meet with Frank
Fini and himself, would I be willing, in Irving Park, where Fini's Ford
dealership was located, Tuesday week, at noon?

[4]

MY FIRST THOUGHT WAS that Fini was dying. My second thought
was that whether he was dying or not, he was heavily drugged.
Third thought: neither. His eyes were quite remarkably large, black
and glazed, almost comical. But beneath the glaze they were burning. His mouth was a straight, thin line, turning down slightly at
each end, his hair thin, too, slight of build, slow and quiet of gesture. He sat in the front seat of a car out on the lot, the door open,
one leg in the car, one out. George Swanson looked like William
Faulkner: a tweed sport coat that looked like he'd gone duck
hunting in, bristly white hair, black eyebrows, little black mustache, pipe clenched at all times between teeth. He leaned against a
front fender, arms folded, hood open behind him. Big men in union
windbreakers stood in small groups here and there about the lot. I
was introduced to and shook hands with Fini, but he said nothing;
I couldn't tell if he was looking at me impassively, or not looking
at me at all. Swanson broke my personal space quite suddenly. He
came in very close and stared at my breastbone. He took his pipe
out of his mouth only to point with it.

15

"Lots of things," he said, smiling at my breastbone and then with an almost audible click deeply into my eyes, "happening all at once. I'm assuming you've got homework to do. Mr. Fini just wanted, you know, to say hello. Are you free this time next week? Yes? Good. Until then. Take care."

[5]

I DID HAVE HOMEWORK to do. The only thing I thought I knew about the mob, at least off the top of my head, was what I'd read in a silly little feature the *Weekly Reader* had run: mob faces on high school yearbook bodies, Most Likely to Succeed, Best Dressed, Personality Plus, and so on, quotes from Shakespeare and the Bible in speech balloons. But the first person I called was my ex, who had moved to Minnesota and was living with a fuzzy-headed Yugoslavian writer who was all the rage. They were pulling in grants right and left, doing what I don't know, but doing very well.

"Dorothy," I said, "I just shook hands with a guy who may become the next boss of Chicago."

She was unimpressed. I knew she would be; that was why I called.

"I remember Chicago," she said, "like this: I go to the bus stop in the morning and without even the benefit of coffee I see, instead of my bus, a hideously butchered corpse. Now you what, want to have lunch with the guy who did it? Yes, I know, you live in Chicago, the mob is cool, it's hip to profess a sociologically based objectivity and secretly adore the violence, pepper it all with sophomoric fin de siècle black humor, and not come right out with embarrassing moral revulsion. But I feel moral revulsion."

"So do I!"

"But what a coup for you!"

"I feel moral revulsion, Dorothy!"

"Then why have anything to do with it?"

"I feel the same way talking to the pizza king."

"It's not the same thing, Jack, and you know it."

"I do *not* know that."

"It's all Ridiculous World, all Entertainment City."

"No, I wonder if a mobster, you know, an organized criminal, might not somehow be apart from that."

"You want to romanticize these murderous, greedy pigs because you have a notion they're not part of Ridiculous World? Of course they're not! They're part of Horrible World! They and I don't know who else, the contras, Hitler types, Newt Gingrich—"

"No, Newt is part of, well, he's the cover boy for Ridiculous World."

"Fine, I get them confused, Ridiculous and Horrible."

"There's a lot of back and forth there. A lot of give, a lot of play. I mean, haven't the contras become glamour boys? They're more suited to that lifestyle than to, like, politics or revolution or even, you know, business, work. Your mobster, on the other hand, is more a businessman, more inclined—"

"To see what he does as a transaction rather than a violation, as an act of honor rather than dishonor? Whereas the people in Horrible World know they are violating some standard, some principle, if only to set up their own system of transaction—making, though, the mobster part of Ridiculous World, no?"

"I don't know, it gets murky, doesn't it?"

"When Newtie says that the contras won, he's just being a spokesperson, right? A P.R. guy, right? But for whom? For the masters of Horrible World? Or is Horrible World after all just a particularly lifelike and effective amusement within the theme park that is Ridiculous World?"

"I don't know. I'll write this book, then run for Congress, and then maybe I'll know."

"Good-bye, Jack. Be careful. This has happened before."

She hung up before I could clarify the last remark. I was convulsed with hubris and maybe that was what she meant. I hardly ever knew what she meant, and certainly did not understand why we were no longer married. Hubris? It came upon me suddenly. I swore I would not write some mock-sophisticated infotainment for a global media empire, but rather a very great and timeless book. I swore, calmly and soberly, something to the effect of nailing them all, pizza king and mob kingpin, I would track fraudulence and arrogance and cruelty and greed into the heart of darkness, the deepest, blackest hell on the globe, the soul of the American taxpayer—and I would do it all for my ex-wife, strangely enough, she who had become so frightened she could no longer dance, could hardly move, she for whom I had always labored to be brave and relentless and name and indict the great villains of our time.

I got a fresh notebook out from the closet and wrote on the cover with a felt-tip pen, NOTES FOR BOOK ON CHICAGO MOB. I believed I would find out who the next boss of the city would be, strip him naked, and throw the soiled garments of his Terror in the face of Amused America—and, in the swift and brilliant progress of this action, become rich and famous. Maybe even hook up with a new wife, better even than Dorothy! Because my first note was *very lonely*. Second note, after some scotch, though I am not much of a drinker: *All systems of order are suspect, the only one free of corruption is death—the ultimate corruption, ironically.*

[6]

I COULD NOT BRING MYSELF to say the words out loud: *rich, famous, sexually powerful*. But I thought them. They appeared in my mind and I batted them aside, from *me* to *not-me*. Then I called a friend at the City News Bureau.

"*Fini* called you? Fini *called* you? Fini," he finished, "called *you?*"

"Yes."

"Something is surely up with Fini. Dark side of the moon."

"He looked, I don't know, unwell."

"This guy Ferriola, he recently failed to survive heart surgery. DeBakey, right? Sinatra referred him. It no longer matters who he knew. Everything in Chicago is supposed to be up for grabs. I hear Berlusconi, I hear Puppo, I hear Fini. I should say I did hear Fini but I no longer hear Fini. Jack, you got great timing. You want to go to Indiana with me, dig some bodies out of a shallow grave?"

I took a train downtown, made my way through the halogen haze of lower Wacker, met my friend, and departed for Indiana.

[7]

IN A CORNFIELD, WE SPOKE to an old man who was the county sheriff, and observed the disinterment of two men. They had been lying there for no more than, it was guessed, three or four days. But what a difference a day can make! Decomposition had not much obscured the nature and effects of their fatal woundings, but it had begun to. Mostly the men no longer looked real. They were parti-colored and as bloated as characters in a cartoon. Wearing only boxer shorts, one of them looked so much like Moe of the Three Stooges that we couldn't help but fix him with that name. His brother (they were brothers, I was told) we called Larry.

"Curly alone survived," I said.

"What puzzles me," said the sheriff, "is lookit this now, they buried 'em, say, four nights ago. There was a full moon that night!" He glared at us from under the bill of his cap, as if we'd done it and were damn fools. "I can't believe they'd work so close to the road like this when the moon was up there like a spotlight shining on their little show. And lookit this, their hole cuts into this row of corn." He lumbered over and examined a stalk, fingering the leaves not like a policeman but a farmer. "The farmer cannot help but notice such an

incursion. Why would they be so stupid is what I want to know."
He looked at us now as if we were doing some kind of special TV
segment on him. Tassels behind him seemed to wave atop his cap,
as if it were adorned with them, some Hessian decoration pluming
golden, the sun setting, everything on fire from there to the horizon,
our faces red as if burned, two heaps of stinking, smear-featured
flesh at our feet. "Of course they wanted them to be discovered,"
said the sheriff, looking sadly off down the road.

Flies thickened on the walls of the hole. We could hear them, and
the black earth seemed to be moving as if we could not see it clearly
through a windblown veil. "Gorging on the seepage," said the sheriff.

After a while I said, "You mean the flies."

[8]

IN MY NOTEBOOK I WROTE *I am learning things I do not want to
know.* Spent a few days rubbing my eyes and listening to the whir and
click of microfilm machines, reading everything I could find on Frank
Fini. He was your basic hoodlum, it seemed, no more, no less. *I am
learning nothing I want to know.* Looked at some pictures of a much
younger Fini, from the mid-1950s. It could easily have been another
man entirely. I stared for a long time at the photographs, and at the two
notes I'd written. Before I knew it, Tuesday had rolled around again.

[9]

FINI AND SWANSON AND THE BIG MEN in windbreakers were exactly as I had left them. But the air was troubled in a new way. Maybe it
was only my knowledge that Fini was no longer being spoken of, whatever that might actually mean. Swanson greeted me like a sportsman
and opened a door to the back seat. A big man in a windbreaker got in

from the other side. Swanson buckled in behind the wheel, saying that he liked to drive, while Fini, next to him in the front, quietly lit a cigarette. Dragging wanly, he unfolded a pair of sunglasses and put them on his face, working the stems carefully, as if afraid of poking himself in the eye. He cleared his throat, but said nothing. Swanson, the big man, and I exhaled at the same time. We pulled out of the lot and drove for a long time. Finally I asked where we were going.

Swanson inclined his head slightly back toward me. I could see the bowl of his pipe and smell it, though there was no tobacco burning in it. "Mr. Fini's restaurant, for an early dinner. It's the Rosebud, on Taylor. Do you know it?"

"Um, no, I guess I don't, what is that, must be about what—?"

"Fifteen hundred west."

"Fifteen hundred west, no, haven't been out that way much recently."

"The old neighborhood."

"What is it exactly," I said venturesomely, "that I can do for you gentlemen?"

Nobody said anything for another period of time I judged overlong. I had not, prior to this moment, believed myself to be frightened. The morgue frightened me, but these men, so persuasively associated with death, did not. In keeping with this belief I had produced for their enjoyment a professional persona, friendly but nononsense, serious but skeptical, sincere but hard-boiled, a reporter's reporter, a bargainer in good faith, using a vocabulary of words and gestures—and a mask—that were as solidly associated, in the proper consciousness, with the man I wanted them to think I was as their code words and fashions were with sudden and nonchalant violence. I thought I would appear before them in a good light, which would help me get what I wanted, but which turned out to be a light specifically designed to ward off evil.

But if what I'd done in posing such a falsely offhand question was to announce my fear, the other three men in the car only seemed bored by it. After a moment, Fini lit another cigarette. With the first drag, he inhaled fully half of it. I watched the cherry burn toward his lips.

Swanson said, "Look, do us a favor and yourself one in the process and don't get wise, all right? The three of us in this automobile, we've had pros get wise with us for roughly . . . one hundred years combined. That's what?" Swanson did the arithmetic in his head. "Two hundred thousand man-hours of jerks mouthing off, of pretending they're Douglas Fairbanks Jr. or some-goddamn-body. Who'm I thinking of? Errol Flynn? Gable? Pulling their dicks out and hooting. And that's figuring from a normal forty-hour workweek. Double that. You see, Jack? We don't need to hear it from you just now, old man."

He turned around with his elbow crooked over the seat back and grinned at me. I heard his teeth click around the stem of his pipe. I heard the crackle of Fini's cigarette. I heard the rumbling bowels of the big man next to me, who was sweating profusely. I chanced a look at him, pretending interest in a woman walking along the sidewalk: just a kid.

"Nearly half a million hours of penny-ante commentary from wiseguys!" shouted Swanson. "Isn't that amazing? I think that's absolutely amazing!"

He could have been talking about anything in American life. And the Age of Information had only just begun.

I suppose in the back of my mind, even after I had declared myself a frightened and ordinary man, I suspected I was acting, subsuming myself in a role in a search for truth—that after all was my abominably comic modus operandi, adapting myself, to the point of mimicked dialect in some cases, dangerous parody of same in others, to my surroundings, doing it without thinking, never thinking about the fact that I wasn't thinking, preferring to believe I was simply going about my duties calmly and methodically. But if the question is had I rehearsed or was I improvising, hindsight suggests I was improvising. And to improvise well, to do it properly, you must be able to think on your feet and have lots of energy at your disposal. Slow down for a second and the audience is all over you with rotten fruit. I *could* think on my feet—it was my one truly reportorial skill—and, because I was frugal with it, had energy to burn. In this way I believe I fooled myself into thinking I was in control. But in the back of my mind, well, yes, sure, there sat the fool, shooting glances right and left.

The rest of the ride was a kind of epiphany. Most people of accomplishment secretly believe, some of the time anyway, that they are deceiving those around them. I cannot say so with authority, but I don't think I was too far wrong—the effectiveness of the pose, the violent consequences for anyone attending that pose notwithstanding—in ascribing to Fini, and to a lesser degree to Swanson as well, that sense of ludicrous theatricality, of histrionic deceit. And I thought, I have nothing to lose but my life. If I can see the loss of my life as the proper and natural end to a certain course of events, then I actually have nothing to lose. I *am* acting. I have never done anything *but* act. Death is merely the end of the act, and who does not acknowledge the need for the end?

[10]

WHEN WE GOT TO THE ROSEBUD, the big man got out, opened Fini's door, opened Swanson's door, and, interestingly, opened my door. I thanked him and a limo pulled up behind us. From its dark interior two young men emerged, twins, muscular, good-looking, one with his left arm in a sling, the other his right, followed by two women, blondes, similar-looking but not twins and with no bones obviously broken.

"Mr. Fini," said one young man.

"Mr. Fini," said the other.

Fini nodded at them, wearily validating their heads-up recognition of him. His shoulders were hunched as if against cold, and the cigarette disappeared quickly into his mouth. A parking valet jogged into our midst, jingling with keys, but the big man had already pulled away from the curb.

"Hello, Mr. Fini, good to see you again, how are you?" the valet enunciated winningly. Swanson handed him some money and the kid jogged off with a salute and smile.

We entered a blood-red darkness. I could see nothing for an agonizingly long time. Then I made out a woman, the bottom half of her face lit up by a tiny light on her lectern, as if she were holding a flashlight below her chin. Behind her was a large framed photograph of Frank Sinatra shaking the hand of a younger but recognizable Frank Fini. As my eyes adjusted, I saw the line for tables was quite long, and the bar was three and four deep. Bach cello suites vibrated under the buzz and grate of conversation. We walked slowly past the people waiting in line, tough-looking men, important-looking men. The mayor looks like a mobster and the mobster looks like a mayor. Beautiful women, exhausted and frightened. Everyone must wait.

Every third or fourth man touched Fini's elbow in silent greeting, but Fini could do little more than lift his chin or shrug. The look on his face was, unmistakably, one of deepening confusion. I saw silk shirts and gold chains and white trousers, conservatively cut suits with ties knotted like tiny fists at the throats of men working on contemptuous pouts and sneers beneath merrily deadly eyes. Swanson and I sat down at a table and Fini wandered off, like a little boy.

"My *client*," said Swanson, "is on the threshold of *a new life*. If not altogether a *dream*."

I said that I saw, and smiled nervously, on and off, like a light.

"*What*," asked Swanson, "do you *think* you know about my *client*?"

I didn't like the way he was exaggerating the word *client*. "I know," I said, "what you'd expect me to know."

"Like for instance!"

24

"Oh," I said (the resemblance of Swanson to Faulkner was so striking in the low red light of the restaurant that I found it disturbing that he didn't have a countertenor Mississippi accent: it took me a second to actually hear what he was saying), "the Fey Manning Department Store shootout, the missing fingers, the Charles Gross murder."

"My *client* is a much more interesting and complex man than his rap sheet and clippings make him out to be."

"I see. I guess most people feel that way."

"The bottom line is he feels very fortunate and he wants to give something back."

"I don't quite . . . what do you mean? Taxes?"

Swanson raised his glass of bourbon and drank it off. "Jack," licking his lips, "where did you go to school?"

"Coe College, in Iowa, class of—"

"Coe! Are you kidding me? Coe?"

"Class of '77."

"CLASS OF '50!"

"Oh really," I smiled.

"REALLY!"

"Coe," I repeated firmly.

"Oh this is great! Coe!"

He signaled for another bourbon. "Two," he said to the waiter. "Drink with me, Jack." I couldn't quite tell if it was a plea or a command. "And bring Mr. Fini's package to me, thank you, Paul. Coe College. Imagine that! Dear old Coe. I was on the table tennis, the bowling, and the golf squads. Those were the best years of my life. I felt lucky to be getting a college education. When I graduated, however, oops, no job, no prospects, no friends in high places, no contacts. I was a farm boy with a pregnant wife. We moved to Saint Paul, Minnesota, and I went to law school at night, Billy Mitchell Law. Do you know Saint Paul? I miss Saint Paul. Got out of Billy Mitchell, same situation as before, but with a law degree. We came here in '54. I went into this old church, and I got down on my hands and knees, Jack, hands and knees, and I said, Sweet Jesus, dear Lord, Christ my Savior, please help me in this my hour of need. I have no friends in high places, and so on. I have a wonderful wife and the cutest little daughter a man could dream of having, and they are counting on me, Lord, on me alone. Grant unto me a *client*, O Lord, and ten thousand in fees the first fiscal year and you can leave the rest to me. And I came out of that church into the blinding light of a summer afternoon in Chicago and who should bowl me out of the way but the Fini brothers! Bring us two of the usual, Paul, and two more drinks, thank you, let me finish my story here, Jack, and then we'll get to the package. Where was I? Blinding light of—right, John Fini slaps Frank on the back of the head and bellows, You gotta get a fuckin' lawyer now! And Frankie says ah fuck you. I've got my hand—Thank you, Paul, that was quick, keep 'em coming like that why don't you—hand over heart, which is beating like a tom-tom, and one hand over my eyes so that I can see who's talking, they're just shapes lost in the glare of the sidewalk until I put my hand up, and then I say in my most professional voice, I'm a lawyer, maybe I can be of some assistance." Swanson chugged his bourbon. "Rest is history." He handed the package across the table to me. I am no drinker and so was already very drunk. I sang the first few words of "Happy Birthday," and cut the string with my steak knife, unwrapped the heavy paper, and found a manuscript: *A Boy's First Book of Mobsters,* by Frank Fini, as told to George Swanson.

"Read it and let me know what you think, next Tuesday noon, at the lot."

When I stepped out of the Rosebud, the sun was setting, blazing down the street. It was a moment of ominous conflagration. I felt, and thought I saw, out of the corner of my eye, that people were running toward me from the west, fleeing some disaster, perhaps screaming in their fear, but I couldn't sort the sounds quickly enough, and when I turned to look the nightmare fully in the face, there was only a skateboarder and the parking valet I'd seen before, running for a car.

[11]

EVERYONE AROUND ME in the restaurant had been tough and beautiful. I suppose I felt the allure of being tough and beautiful, as well as rich and famous. I felt dizzy and stupid with these thoughts, and I liked the feeling. The danger involved in an unstable person assuming a role is that it might not be shucked in time to avert embarrassment, an overshooting of the target, the goal of the assumption, its purpose—or a falling short, a falling off into confusion and melodrama, the comedy a farce. The actor becomes a toy of plot. The moment takes on qualities it cannot hold. It shatters, it rusts, it becomes infested with the brilliant mold of failure. I turned to *A Boy's First Book of Mobsters* with a sense of creeping fuzziness.

The best thing about it was the title; the rest was like a ghosted showbiz bio, or the story of some sporting hero's hard life and eventual transmogrification—except that it detailed "a life of crime." For example:

"When I was a very small boy, I had a strong desire to own a horse, a desire I shared with many young children. With me, though, it was different. *I had to have the pony.* (This was a time, I should point out, when there were still horses to be found here and there around Chicago!) I located one that I liked and without a second thought, stole it. My uncle had a garage and I brought the pony there, fearing the beating I was sure to get if I showed up at home with it. I was never so happy as I was that day. I opened the doors to the sidewalk lift and took myself and my pony to the basement. Then I set about the task of finding or stealing some food for it. While I was out, my uncle surprised the pony—or I should say the pony surprised my uncle! In either case, she reared up and struck at him—so he swore—and my uncle shot her dead, in self-defense. Because I had caused so much trouble, not only was I confronted with a dead pony but the job of getting that dead pony out of the basement and over to the butcher's. I certainly learned a lot about life and business from my uncle, but I never forgave him. How could I? He'd broken my heart and I didn't believe him. Of course I soon found myself in situations where I was forced to take measures as strong as, and in many cases much stronger than, killing a child's pony, but no, I never forgave him. You see, he was a coward after all. (Later facts confirmed what I had suspected as a child.) Only a coward would shoot a horse like that, for no good reason. Or a fool. And that is precisely what I told him he was when I killed him, many years later, tears staining the hands that choked the life from his body."

There were other moving episodes: births, baptisms, weddings, funerals, all of these events featuring superb entertainment by top-name performing artists, all of whom were close personal friends. "I never forgot, however, that they were whores. Let us face facts: I fucked them or they fucked me, whatever, and I paid them. I never respected them fully. Not the least reason was that I could sing pretty well myself and knew flat from sharp! One asshole tried to tell me that he was not a whore, and he made me so mad I started choking him. I stuffed many thousands of dollars into his mouth and ripped his pants off before I came to my senses and was dragged away by my lieutenants and attorney."

One of his favorite whores was Wayne Newton because Newton had little embossed cards on all the tables for his shows that informed audience members of Mr. Newton's expectations: a standing ovation. They were asked, with a little exclamation point, not to disappoint him! "People take that kind of shit. It goes a long way toward explaining the whys and wherefores of my way of life, I think."

Wrote in my notebook *Reads like script for lounge act and official biography of the president of the United States of America. Grinning sleaze and unimaginable power.*

[12]

I MADE MY NOON APPOINTMENT at Fini Ford, but neither Fini nor Swanson was there, and the big men in windbreakers refused to acknowledge my presence. The little plastic banners strung around the lot snickered in the breeze. A salesman asked what kind of car I liked. I refused to acknowledge him. It would be two months before I heard again from Swanson.

[13]

TRANSCRIPT OF CONVERSATION WITH BERNARD GUMMER, *CHICAGO TRIBUNE*, APRIL 3RD, 1989

GUMMER: That thing on?

ME: Yes, I think so. Can you tell me, first of all, do you still believe as you mentioned on the phone that based on the information you've gotten that uh, that Frank Fini is probably the new top guy?

GUMMER: *Yes I do.* I do and I'll tell you *why* I do. Sam "Burly" Berlusconi, who suddenly has been considered a heavyweight, is merely a chauffeur and, uh, more or less a lackey for Joey Puppo, who is better known in mob circles as "Yo-yo Brain," as he used to fight under that name many years ago. Prizefighter. Of course you know he's in prison now, with a long sentence and in poor health. Rochester, where the uh, the uh Mayo Clinic is, the Federal Correction Center there. Berlusconi, who got the nickname "Wings" in addition to "Burly" because he flies so much, all over, as a courier. *As a courier,* now that would in fact make him something of a heavyweight, I grant you, because he's privy to a lot of mob secrets. He has to tell one mob guy what another mob guy has to say, and they have to respect his orders, quote close-quote, his instructions quote close-quote, or else they would not adhere to them. But he's an older guy and what with the animals we have in organized crime today . . . !

ME: They weren't animals before, you're saying . . . ?

GUMMER: Not like this, no sir. Today you have to be damn tough! And *Frank Fini is known* as a tough guy, quote close-quote, a stand-up guy.

ME: A stand-up guy?

GUMMER: That's a guy who would go to prison before he would make a deal, implicate his colleagues in the mob.

ME: So loyalty is important.

GUMMER: Very much so.

ME: What about there being no honor among thieves?

GUMMER: Well, sure, that's a problem, but by and large, in quote close-quote the good old days, loyalty was paramount.

ME: And with the animals of today, loyalty has less of a place?

GUMMER: To a degree. Certainly it's more complicated.

ME: Loyalty is?

GUMMER: Yes. The game is much bigger and more subtle.

ME: I mean, the sense of mutual aid, if you will, that they might have looked to in the past, you know, to put it in the best light—they were like a guild, a brotherhood, a union if you like, they could count on each other like, well, like good anarchists, maybe, and contract—no pun intended—negotiate with outside groups, and now maybe they can't. Can't look to each other in that way anymore.

GUMMER: Well, frankly, I don't know about all that.

ME: Let's get back to Fini.

GUMMER: Background as a burglar. Almost every one of the top crime syndicate gangsters, with the exception of Anthony Accardo and maybe Paul Ricca who is now dead, had backgrounds as thieves, as holdup guys.

ME: So there's what, stand-up guys and holdup guys?

GUMMER: Bank robbers and yeah, right, guys who have committed violent crimes.

ME: Coercion rather than negotiation then.

GUMMER: That's how you come to the attention of mob leaders.

ME: So it's authoritarian rather than—

GUMMER: You have to show how you can enforce the rules. A violent crime is simply a credential. Instead of a Ph.D., you break some guy's head open.

ME: It looks to me like Fini's credential might have been this Charles Gross murder. Do you—

GUMMER: I do indeed! I recall the case very vividly! Charles Gross was acting ward committeeman for the Thirty-first Ward. His counterpart was Thomas Kean, the alderman who later went to jail. The gist of it was this: Dan Roberts was the uh, the guy in the Thirty-first, and he wanted to get out. Wanted to become a judge. Gross took his place. Now Tom Kean's ward was a target for a takeover by the mob. They were hoping to wrest control of the city council by getting their own honchos in spots like alderman and ward committeeman.

ME: That's interesting.

GUMMER: What is?

ME: Political aspiration.

GUMMER: Well, sure.

ME: It's not the first thing you think of when you think about the mob.

GUMMER: All part of a day's work. Now Kean, he had been threatened by the mob. Gross consulted Kean on the matter and was told not to worry quote close-quote about it. But this guy over in the Twenty-eighth, George Kells, his precinct captains all had their fingers broken with nutcrackers because Kells had been told to move aside and hadn't. So Gross, short story, decided to defy the crime syndicate! He was walking down Kedzie thinking it was a movie or some goddamn thing like that, and a car pulled up, looked like a squad car and probably was, and witnesses said somebody put a spotlight on him. Near that small church there. When Gross hesitated, *shotgun-wielding executioners blew him to bits!* Now the irony, wait, the irony is that he had just been to the *Sun-Times* asking that a story about his being threatened be held until he was sure it was a serious threat! Until he had more information!

ME: I guess he got all the info he could handle.

GUMMER: Let that be a lesson to you.

ME: I've heard they don't kill journalists.

GUMMER: They kill whoever they feel like killing.

ME: I see.

GUMMER: Tell Jake Lingle they don't kill reporters. Took a bullet in the head from a snub-nosed .38 in 1930. More recently, Victor Reisel had acid thrown in his face. And this guy in Arizona, Don somebody? Was blown up in his car. Bolles. Don Bolles. Yes, the Gross story was my first big story. They had a hundred suspects. Never went to trial. Poor goddamn Gross. I knew his wife. Knew his son.

ME: So that was the first time you—

GUMMER: First time I saw Frank "Fingers" Fini. Do you know why they call him "Fingers"?

ME: No, I do not.

GUMMER: Because he had two of them blown off the first time I ever made his acquaintance. Got a call from a source. It was eleven p.m. on November something, lemme think, just after his birthday, right around Thanksgiving, in the year nineteen hundred and forty-nine. A team of crack Chicago police detectives is cruising the Loop, looking for the Three Minute Gang, so named because legend had it they could clear out a store in the time it takes to poach an egg. They were just across the river at what used to be the Fey Manning women's wear shop, and they noticed the beam of a flashlight cut across the sidewalk. They drove down to the lower level and found a rear door jimmied. They entered the building, ascended a flight of stairs, and were confronted by a young man, just turned twenty-one, named Frank Fini. Fini fired three shots from a .45 automatic. Now there is some contention about the caliber, the weapon. I happen to believe it was a 7.654 milli German automatic, and was used to kill a saloon owner not a year earlier. But my pal, Detective Lieutenant Russell Just, dropped Fini in his tracks with a bullet to the stomach region. Other shots were fired as well, and Fini lost a couple of fingers. Next day I visited him in his hospital room, in the company of Just and Fini's brother John. Johnny says to Frank, "You know you caused Ma to have a heart attack this morning," to which Frank replies, "Too bad!"

ME: I see what you mean by "tough guy."

GUMMER: Tough? He was cool as a cucumber. Night before he's lying in a pool of his own blood and all he can think to say is, Nice shot, Lieutenant!

ME: And you think, you're pretty well convinced, that this is the guy who's going to be the next uh, next boss of Chicago?

GUMMER: That is who I am going with, yes sir.

ME: Let me ask you, how did you come to that conclusion?

GUMMER: This little black book here. You know, I once reached a major crime figure while he was sitting on the crapper in his yacht in the Caribbean.

ME: You mean he told you he was sitting—

GUMMER: *These guys don't care what I think of them!* Why should they care what *I* think? They do *not* care what I think.

ME: Okay, but I do. I'm wondering what your advice is regarding contacting Fini and, uh, talking to him.

GUMMER: Jack, what are you, nuts? No, *do not try to contact Fini.* You have no idea—Look, maybe after you've been doing this for several decades and people know you, maybe you can—I mean, when you know *good* guys from *bad* guys and have *friends*—But until such time do not, repeat *do not* stick your nose in where it's likely to get shot off. Quote close-quote.

ME: Well, okay, thanks for the—

GUMMER: Wait, before you go, this, this is, hang on, this is Fini's number I'm dialing now, lemme see what I can, hang on, seven, nine, see what I can do for you—Darn, it's just saying it's a recording, it's just saying the cellular customer is out of range.

END OF TRANSCRIPT

[14]

I CAME AWAY FROM THE INTERVIEW with Gummer thinking about the etymology of "mob": *mobile vulgus,* the vacillating crowd, democracy, and how organized crime was not so much the evil twin of anarchism, all against all in a pure freedom à la Stirner, but really just undisguised democratic capitalism. The operative word was "organized"; the "crime" was neither here nor there. Gummer told the tragic story of the slain alderman with a wife and son, the funny story of the infamous butcher pooping in the blue bedazzling Caribbean, but it was the day-in, day-out stuff that made up most of the real story, the small-time greed of "men with families," the political power plays in which occasionally violence was done, the whining gears of the mechanisms of local politics, the chuff chuff chuffing of fat men overworking their hearts—That was what the mob in Chicago was all about, I thought, that and the relentless banality of *A Boy's First Book of Mobsters.* I began to think dispiritedly that I was "on the trail" of just another guy who wanted to publish a memoir of how he'd succeeded in business. I would have walked at that point if I had not remembered that all politics is local, and that the little gears were connected to bigger gears.

[15]

GERRY NELSON IS THE CHIEF INVESTIGATOR for the Chicago Crime Commission. Medium height and weight, little bit of a belly hard over the belt when he "doffs his jacket," pleasant blue eyes, short, wispy brown hair, a church usher's suit and demeanor. Knowing how many mobsters he'd stood up to, I was mesmerized by his nearly invisible wall-floweriness. His office is on West Monroe above the Bell Federal Savings Bank, and when I was shown in, he was bent over an organizational flow chart of mob management, shifting names with the *plack* sounds of little magnets adhering. Fini, he told me, had moved up on the chart from foot soldier to crew boss in charge of rackets in Melrose Park, Elmwood Park, Park Forest, and various western suburbs, many years earlier. He had been definitely connected to Jimmy Hoffa, but in what way connected and to what end was not clear. He had spent two years in Cuba and five in Las Vegas. Then suddenly he was back in Chicago. Nobody knew exactly when he'd returned; suddenly he was there, and the rumors were to the effect that he had changed, was in some mysterious way no longer the Frank Fini he'd been when he left. Very much a presence in day-to-day mob affairs, he appeared to have no stake in them. His attention was elsewhere. His stock only seemed to rise as a result.

Nelson sighed and showed me some photos: Fini face down in a black pool of blood at the Fey Manning; Fini with a look on his face like the marshal holding onto Oswald as Ruby drills him, one cop grabbing Fini's knees, another his elbow cocked high for a punch, a third with his head set way back on his neck, eyes wide open, double chin as big as a softball, hat an inch above his head, like a halo; a wryly contemplative Fini, sitting on the curb, flipping the photographer the bird, the effect made comic by the absence of most of the finger; Fini looking at a pal who had just been paralyzed in the proverbial hail of gunfire; and Fini in the Gross lineup. Then he stopped being available for photographs.

35

TRANSCRIPT OF CONVERSATION WITH GERRY NELSON, CHI-
CAGO CRIME COMMISSION, APRIL 10TH, 1989

NELSON: Fini. Fini is not one of the guys we follow now, with
any regularity. Maybe we've been very wrong about him, but he
seems like a celebrity greeter to us. Anti-greeter, I guess I should say.
He was arrested some twenty-seven times, convicted four times on
minor charges. Mainly a burglar and a collector of debts, street tax,
and so on. He went away for seven years and came back. He meets
people now. He . . . well, look, the mob might not scare you, as a
concept, but Frank Fini most definitely would. Scares the poop out of
me. And I don't mean to imply he's just some massive intimidating
bonehead. He has real presence. But he doesn't seem to do anything
of real importance.

ME: Do you suspect he's maybe just under your radar?

NELSON: It's a reasonable suspicion, but no. We do not suspect he's connected to anything important. We think he may be a
decoy, a centerpiece. Something like that.

ME: Some people I've talked to think he's a strong candidate.

NELSON: Like I said, we may have been very wrong about
Mr. Fini. All I can tell you is that the last thing he did of note was
twenty-five years ago.

ME: Which was . . . ?

NELSON: Ex-con Joe Wiesphal refuses to make the exorbitant
payments demanded of him on his juice loan. Fini and friends take
Wiesphal to a cooler in the basement of Mr. Lucky's Tavern on West
Belmont, handcuff him to a beam, put a pot on his head, and beat it
until his ears bled. Then they beat him with a nightstick, choked him
with an electrical cord, and propped him up in a booth upstairs as
an example to other borrowers. Case goes to trial and ends with the
acquittal of Fini and friends. We wondered how such an acquittal was
possible and found that Fini owned many, many persons in law enforcement, including but not limited to the state's attorney and a number

of judges. This was when we thought he was still a crew boss. Then he left town. Didn't come back for seven years. We think he got a little ahead of himself and lost his way. We think Berlusconi is the new guy.

ME: The chauffeur.

NELSON: That's right. This is a car culture, after all. Guy didn't get lost.

END OF TRANSCRIPT

[16]

MY OFFICE WAS A ROOM the size of a walk-in closet, made even smaller by three tall bookcases taking up most of the three unwindowed walls. (The window offered a view of Senn High School, if you know Chicago, way uptown, not quite as far as Loyola, down the block from the Gauler houses, if you know architecture.) The books in these cases appeared to have been thrown at them, rather than shelved, and there were high, teetering piles of more books, rising up like stalagmites from the floor. There was a photo of Dorothy dancing, framed with her motto: *The gateway of the mysterious female is called the root of heaven and earth.* From the *Tao Te Ching,* I think. On a card table were phone, tape recorder, and typewriter.

It's possible to feel evil coming at you from a great distance, across a city, invisible in wires strung overhead or braided deep underground, fiber-optically, to see it manifest in the shape of the telephone itself, just before it rings and everything changes. Imagine: all that power, all that money, all that technology—it's impossible that the phone not be a force, that it's a convenience and nothing more.

It rang.

I said my name. It sounded strange to me.

"You know who this is?"

"No, I'm afraid—"

The voice was high-pitched in a kind of nervousness and yet friendly, familiar, with something in it that demanded the acceptance of the intimacy it offered. The demand was clear even in the long silence that ensued, in which we two simply breathed.

"You're in a lot of trouble."

"Am I?"

"Do you know who this is?"

"No, I don't. Who is this?"

"You're in a lot of trouble."

"So I understand."

"God are you stupid."

"Am I?"

The caller hung up, and immediately I called someone I knew in publishing. I described what I was doing and she told me to send what I had.

"Haven't got much."

"Send what you can. Send a tape."

"First chapter is called 'My Wife Leaves Me.'"

"Interesting."

"Second chapter is 'I Learn Things I Do Not Want to Know.'"

"I see!"

"Third is 'I Run Out of Money,' and the fourth is 'Who Do I Think I Am?'"

"Sounds like you're right in the middle of it!" cried my friend. "Gritty and grueling. Everything kind of boiling over, is it? Take care, Jack, stay on top of the horse and if you fall off, just get back on quick as you can, okay, Jack?"

"Okay."

"Okay then."

I let a frightening thought trickle through my brain: that I had let the caliber of my work slip a little, without realizing it, thinking I had my shoulder to the wheel, that the "level of my concern" had dropped down a rung or two or three. It was not, as I had convinced myself, that I had narrowed the scope of my work from national to local because I wanted to understand the politics within the politics within the politics, the ins and outs and days and nights of American lives, no, it came to me as I went over my Nelson notes, and I wrote it down: *Am going to pieces in a calm and methodical way.* I said to myself, Jack old boy, you're out of money, you're going to have to take those credit cards out of the blocks of ice you froze them in, and start tapping.

[17]

TRANSCRIPT OF CONVERSATION WITH DR. ARTHUR PLANT, M.D., LINCOLN PARK, APRIL 24TH, 1989

> PLANT: I do not want to talk to you.
>
> ME: Why not?
>
> PLANT: *I do not want to talk to you!*
>
> ME: Help me understand why not.
>
> PLANT: No. (Pause of five seconds.) Because you are an idiot.
>
> ME: Maybe so, but mainly I'm ignorant.
>
> PLANT: Whatever!
>
> ME: That's why I *need* to talk to you. I need your help.
>
> PLANT: It was twenty-five *years* ago, my friend!
>
> ME: But you remember it like it was yesterday.
>
> PLANT: Why do you want to know this? What happened? Did he die?
>
> ME: No, somebody else died and they think he might be the next boss of Chicago.
>
> PLANT: Oh terrific. That's the kind of man who makes it big in America. We have them in the medical profession as well. Greedy, ruthless jerks. But big, big, big! Why publicize their exploits? Haven't you got anything better to do as a watchdog of liberty?

ME: No. Frankly, no sir, I do not. I believe this business with Frank Fini has larger implications. For the country as a whole. I want to get to the bottom of it, so that I can then, you know, get to the top of it.

PLANT: How much they paying you?

ME: Who do you mean by "they"?

PLANT: Whoever. How much.

ME: I'm freelancing. On spec. I have no book contract, though I certainly hope to in the near future.

PLANT: Nobody's paying you?

ME: No, sir. Frankly, no.

PLANT: Take a big man to admit that.

ME: Thank you.

PLANT: He had a vivid personality.

ME: A real character?

PLANT: Character? No. Character makes him sound fun. Like in a movie. No, he was a profoundly unpleasant man and a thoroughgoing professional. I have met maybe fifty thousand people in my life as a healer. I've talked to lots of tough guys. I was a Marine. But Fini stands out in my mind as being a very tough guy, the toughest guy you'd care to meet. Any tougher than this you don't want to know about it. See what I'm saying? *You do not want to know about it.* That's all I'm saying. He was unhappy. A very tough and unhappy person. I can't do him justice. I think to appreciate how tough and unhappy this guy is you'd have to talk to him, and then you'd run the risk of being killed.

ME: Well, you see, what I'm—I have talked to him. Or should I say I've met him. He didn't actually say a word. His lawyer did all the talking. And I'm having a hard time reconciling the guy I met, who was not what I would call tough—though certainly not without what Gerry Nelson at the Crime Commission calls presence—reconciling that with the guy everybody is describing to me.

NELSON: You arouse my medical curiosity.

ME: Have I got this much right? At the start of the Joseph Wiesphal trial, Frank Fini was hospitalized, claiming injury in an automobile accident. Authorities later discovered that he had simply chosen that weekend to have two pins removed from his ankle. An orthopedic surgeon examined Fini and told the court he was fit to stand trial. You were that surgeon. What did—How did he deal with you after you declared him fit?

PLANT: I got a series of late-night phone calls. Then one fine day I'm underneath my car, working on it, something I used to like to do. I hear footsteps. I say hello? and then BOOM something slams against the car. I see the jack tip and I think, well, that's how it happens for me. The jack collapses and the car comes down, the shocks and springs compress and the oil pan thumps me on the breastbone. Someone calls out to me. I think I recognize the voice as that of Frank Fini. This person asks in a nice, friendly tone, helpful but not overly concerned, "Are you still alive?" I can't think what else to say or do, so I admit it. "Yes," I say, "I am still alive." I can hear the guy squatting so he can talk more discreetly to me. Actually puts his hand on my kneecap. Pats it. "As soon as you people understand it's only because I say so, the better off we'll all be." Jack, I'm sorry I called you an idiot.

ME: That's all right. I am an idiot.

PLANT: No, it's just that you shouldn't be messing around with these guys.

END OF TRANSCRIPT

[18]

STILL IN A PHONE MOOD after the conversation with Dr. Plant, I made an appointment to chat with the FBI, Section Three fellows, wiretappers. I'd been told they knew everything, and used their information like gossip columnists. It was exciting, even after my years at Chicago News Bureau, to hear the receptionist say, "Good morning, Federal Bureau of Investigation. How may I direct your call?" While I was being transferred, a taped voice told me—this was the dawn of that technology, please remember—that my conversation might be recorded for purposes of quality control.

We met, three special agents and myself, at six in the morning in a government cafeteria in the sub-basement of a nondescript office building out near O'Hare. The walls were shockingly, unaccountably painted blood red. Small printed notices were thumbtacked neatly, squarely to a bulletin board. Whenever I chanced to look up, there was somebody standing there, intently reading these notices. There were even cartoons, but I didn't have the opportunity to enjoy them. The room was packed but quiet, a little bit like a prison mess hall, but carpeted and low-ceilinged. The ceiling was in fact so low, and the room quiet enough with its muted clinking of breakfast silverware, that I could hear the fluorescent lights humming. I began to feel like I didn't know where I was, disoriented is the term, perhaps a little weak. But once I accepted this thought, I realized suddenly (like being slapped in the face when you're asleep: it doesn't hurt but it does wake you up) that I was on to something, that it was important, in FBI culture, to exist in a kind of rigorous, highly structured anomie, to feel isolated and weak, to not know where you were or who you were, but to find in the center of that weakness and confusion a sort of comfort, even strength. And that Frank Fini was or had experienced something like a complementary version of same.

SA Jim Stamp wore a ball cap backwards and appeared no older than thirteen. SA William Cuptate was an older man and faintly aggrieved by it, dressed casually in denim and deck shoes, with the air of an aesthete or even libertine with military bearing or authority. SA Chris Jolley was also no older than thirteen, but wore a suit and tie and had a definite supervisory look working for him. They all looked tired and irritated and refused peremptorily to allow me to take notes of any kind: no tape recording, not even so much as a flip-top notepad. When I asked if it was okay for me to remember what they told me, they all laughed hysterically. I assumed they were going to tell me something interesting and important, and was duly excited and grateful, but they told me absolutely nothing.

"If you can't tell me anything, I'm not sure why you're talking to me at all," I said. (You'll just have to trust me that I'm not making this part up.)

"Trying to lend a hand, wherever we can," said SA Jolley. "We're all on the same side."

"Maybe you could tell me a little about what you do in a general sense. Just to help me understand the context of, you know, what we read in the paper."

Both younger agents turned deferentially to SA Cuptate, who cleared his throat. "All right," he said, "I can tell you about an operation we've just terminated."

"Here's a scoop for ya," said SA Stamp, grinning.

"Red Froti, as you know, is alderman for the First Ward. He does business, a good deal of it mob business, from a corner booth in Counsellor's Row Restaurant. He had his own phone at the table."

The three agents snickered privately at this.

"Moron," said SA Stamp.

"Is he connected to Fini, may I ask?"

"Sure he is," said SA Jolley.

"We installed a camera under a banquette seat just across the aisle from his table, and we tapped his line. Reviewing all the material, which is very tedious and takes up most of our days, we get enough solid evidence to indict him for criminal conspiracy. And, we believe, to convict him."

"Really," I said. "Red Froti."

"That's all we've got time for," said SA Jolley, standing up. "As to your basic question: our information is current as of last night.

Berlusconi oversees and okays all important matters from his place in Barrington Hills."

"So you're convinced it's going to be Berlusconi."

SA Stamp nodded. I thanked them for their time and left the building. A block away, I was startled by a tap on my shoulder. It was SA Stamp. I stopped, and he said, "We think Fini is headed for witness relocation. But it's not like the way everybody else goes into it. It's goofy. We know you met with him. We think you ought to stop doing that."

"Why are you telling me this?"

"I'm a human being."

"Wouldn't you guys *know* if he was headed for—"

"No. Not necessarily." SA Stamp shook his head faintly, smiled, turned, and walked away.

[19]

I BECAME A LITTLE OBSESSIVE and fetishistic over the phone call I could not successfully place. I began to take some comfort in the knowledge that I would never reach Swanson again, that the matter of what I was doing and why would resolve itself. But I could confirm my steadfastness by continuing to attempt to make the call. Seven days in a row I waited until my room began to lose its daylight, then punched in the two numbers Swanson had given me. I let each ring ten times. After a pause to collect myself, I tried them again, letting each phone ring nine times. Then eight, then seven, six, five, four, three, two, and one, one over and over until I could not see the phone and the remote ringing sounded louder and louder, unnaturally amplified, potent and profoundly alarming.

Remaining there, performing those rituals, amorphous and isolated in the darkness—It went a long way toward encouraging in me a feeling of creepy invulnerability: little fingers of inquiry extended with hideous magic for miles and miles, tapping on the doors of empty houses, or maybe on the shoulder of a dead man. Wake up, wake up, there's something I need to ask you. Flesh becomes drawn and translucent, the bone work emerges like the exposed roots of old trees, the famous grinning skull says nothing, topples with a crack from its spine. We are able to feel good, able to regard ourselves in mirrors, but inclined not to, inclined toward melancholy, quiet, misery, inclined to use the mirror to shave or to apply makeup, but never to study . . . and so this gentle, daily conflict keeps us alive, keeps us wanting to be alive. Is that it? We are able to imagine a supreme being and this phenomenal power of imagination humbles us to the point of fervent belief in the supreme being? And because we are so taken with our abilities to imagine and believe, a vast order ensues, the single point of which is to prop us up against the strong but actually quite warm, pleasant, lulling wings of death? (A note: *Fini basking in death or death basking in Fini? Gangster afraid of death like everybody else—seeks to master it rather than ignore it.*)

At the end of the week of phoning, I got a letter in the mail, forwarded from the *Weekly Reader,* sent by Henrique Friend. He wrote: "We talked on the meaning of life a while ago Do you remember?! Chinese guy in my building told me life runs up and down your body You can have more of it or less of it You can work at it and get MORE! I said bro I don't have ANY you know so he said he would help me with a program of breathing exercises. Maybe YOU are interested in this. Ricky Friend (from the morgue, man!)"

EXCERPT FROM TRANSCRIPT OF CONVERSATION WITH HENRIQUE FRIEND, COOK COUNTY MORGUE, FEBRUARY 15TH, 1989

RICKY: So I really care for these people.

ME: You mean for—

RICKY: That's right, man, for the dead ones here. I care for them because they were here once and because they need help. They tell me, Don't think like that because then it's not—because then

45

you don't do your job. They don't mean there's—it's not like you can't care, but if you want to be in this field you have to accept what comes in, and learn the lessons that they teach—but see I *am* helping that person, man. I am.

END OF EXCERPT

[20]

TRANSCRIPT OF CONVERSATION WITH GEORGE SWANSON, HOLIDAY INN, DOWNERS GROVE, MAY 3RD, 1989

SWANSON: Men grow each day. When they're young. Younger than a certain age, and after that they have established patterns of living and thinking that are hard to deny. But they deny them anyway and become perverse. Perhaps, Jack, that is the horror of the world—and not bad service at a place where you have come to expect good, like the Holiday Inn—Here comes the waitress, at last! But in the beginning, men are simply growing. They feel, *naturally*, more and more power every day. And if they don't, if some *asshole* makes them feel weak, or even just *less strong than the day before*, well, doesn't that only make things worse over the long haul? *Miss? Waitress?* Oh gee, I thought she was on her way over here but apparently you have to kidnap her. But where was uh, where, what—You get your strength and your bitterness growing together, growing eventually into some kind of goddamn perversion of the noble thing the guy once was. You agree with me so far, Jack?

ME: I'm confused.

SWANSON: What I'm saying is, they grow every day, men do, they feel power in them, and the question becomes where are they to stop? Where do you say to a smart, powerful man, STOP! YOU CAN GO NO FURTHER! Where, Jack, where do you say that?

ME: Well, you don't say it, the guy says it to himself because there—

SWANSON: What do you know, it worked! This young lady thought I was shouting at her! I'd like the number two breakfast, dear, over easy, bacon very crisp, pumpernickel toast, and some more coffee please.

ME: —because there are other concerns in the guy's mind is all I'm saying, Mr. Swanson. I'll have the same, thank you.

SWANSON: Sure, you can say that. It's a good and it's a reasonable point. But let me make an end run around this philosophy here and get back to my original point which is that you want to watch out, Jack, not, listen to me, not for what you think, not for good violence, mob violence, or whatever Gummer tried to scare you with, but violence at the behest and hands of those sworn to protect and serve. We live in a police state, you know that.

ME: Lady wrote a letter to the editor at *Life* while I was there, in response to a piece I'd written about gated communities and over-policing, and she said, If a police state is what it takes for us to be safe, then so be it!

SWANSON: Well there you go, people are idiots.

ME: They're frightened.

SWANSON: The criminal, the policeman: no difference whatsoever. Or rather, two inseparable elements of the whole, always blending, always in equal proportion. But listen to me, one digression after another, haven't enjoyed conversation this much in years, Jack, honestly. What I want to say to you is this: for reasons of vanity, for reasons of financial gain perhaps, or perhaps for other reasons, my client wants to do business with you. No, no, now, don't make any speeches about who you are and what you do, your altruism and your freedom of the press and whatever, people *aren't* idiots. I am saying we are here now, you can relax with us, we're not the enemy, we're not out to hurt or scare you. And you can take this advice as a token of good faith, as a favor: the cops are the ones you want to regard uneasily from here on in. See, because the cops have two ways of doing business with you, guys like you, in your profession, I mean, who, as they see it, are fishing off their pier. Two ways: one is to tell you, a guy for whom they maybe have a *need* but no *respect*, all about a guy whom they are, say, about to indict. You do all the publicity work for them, see? So when the arrest comes down, the deed's value has been amplified or *inflated* beyond its *real* value. So if they're telling you something about, for instance, Frank Fini, hey, it's Fini, psst, hey, publicity boy, it's Fini, you should think twice. Half the time if they're saying it's so-and-so, it means they got a great case and want some fame. The other half of the time it means they're looking in reality at some other figure.

ME: Okay, but—

SWANSON: Number two possibility is that they are feeding you a line. Certain investigators of my acquaintance will take you aside like you're somebody and say, It's Frank Fini we're after, buddy, pal, respected newspaperman. *Just to keep you out of their hair,* see? It's Joe Blow they're really after! *And here is the point the point the point.* Here is the *favor,* Jack. If you go clodhopping around with your notebook, talking to Tom, Dick, and Harry, and you learn something, actually think you've learned something about Figure Z and you report it like a good little reporter, Figure Z starts to worry maybe, puts his car up on the rack to check for bugs, *finds one,* and poof goes the great investigation and possible airtight case! And then, buddy, those detectives will be all over you. You can't beat the kind of fucking they'll give you, because it's legal. Run you out of town? They'll run you out of the country.

ME: Okay, but—

SWANSON: Jack, we are who you want to talk to. Forget about the cops and the pundits. Who are they? What do they know? Who are they talking about to you? Cerone? Jackie the Lackey! Tony Accardo? Mike Linfante? John DiFronzo? Rocco Infelice? Dom Cortina? Sammy Berlusconi? Donald "the Wizard of Odds" Angelini? Did you know that Joe Batters—that's Accardo—was Capone's bodyguard? *Al Capone, for Christ's sake!* I'm dealing with the Reagan administration and the contras and they're still gossiping about Al Capone! Sam Carlisi, by the way, is the guy who's gonna be there at the end of the day. Here in Chicago, I mean. There, you see? I can't keep anything from you, Jack! Can't you see it? I'm your gold mine!

END OF TRANSCRIPT

[21]

I STILL, AT THAT POINT, could not say what it was, exactly, that Fini and Swanson wanted from me. The mention of the Reagan administration, of course, convinced me to see it through, whatever it was. Swanson had babbled about "notes" he was "putting together" for a "companion piece," making repeated references to Schopenhauer; when I got home, I found an old book and read all the passages I'd underlined ten years earlier: "Ultimately we become acquainted with ourselves as quite different from what *a priori* we considered ourselves to be; and then we are quite often alarmed at ourselves." This passage, understandably, brought me up short. This is not the place, and I am not the writer, for a study of Schopenhauer, but what I found myself reading seemed, how shall I say, ominously important: we have free will only insofar as we are able to think we have free will. We are free to think so, to pretend we do, to act as if we do. But in reality we, like a tree, a mayfly, a rock, exist strictly according to our natures, which are revealed more and more fully over the course of time. "In particular, what is bad in the character will come out more and more powerfully with time." I flipped through a hundred pages and was about to set the book aside when I came across the following lines, in which I heard quite clearly the echo of Swanson's voice: "Repentance always results from corrected knowledge, not from a change in the will, which is impossible. Pangs of conscience over past deeds are anything but repentance; they are pain at the knowledge of oneself in one's own nature."

I cannot tell you why, but when I read those words and heard that echo, I was seized by a kind of fear I had never before experienced in my amazingly sheltered life, a rare, nameless fear that rooted me to the spot and drained me of myself in the blink of a magician's eye: it was the fear, as another philosopher, Montaigne, put it, that dreads even help.

I decided to drop the project.

[22]

ACCORDING TO MY NOTES, two mores weeks went by without word from Fini and Swanson. I have no recollection of how I spent the time: probably reading Schopenhauer and Montaigne, and I must have made a copy of *A Boy's First Book of Mobsters,* because my friend in publishing did receive such a manuscript—but I have no memory of sending it. I suppose I struggled with my fear by thinking of the rewards. Then, on the fifteenth night, Swanson appeared in my bedroom.

I had been dreaming I was looking out a window of some remote cabin at a dark woods. I was certain someone was coming toward me in that darkness, and I did not want to be surprised, so I stared intently. Then I turned around and saw a man sitting on a chair in a far corner of the room. I looked at his face for a long, long time. I recall it as resembling Van Gogh's self-portrait in green. The man sat in a cone of light under a gooseneck lamp pulled close, so that his stubbly hair looked white as ash.

The assault in the bedroom in the middle of the night is of course the perfect assault: the hot, nervous, rigidly trained brain finally loosens its hold, the limbs of the sleeper settle, the heart slows, reality flows through the mind, and the sleeper watches it but cares very little, does not seek to order what he sees, nor to control it, expects nothing from it, is at peace with the million swarming forms of disguise . . . and then something happens, a false note is struck, Abraham has killed Isaac, there was no intervention, perhaps there is no God after all, there is nothing that can be done to bring the boy back to life, the web of tiny assumptions that allowed you to think without thinking you were you is torn, the thing that you thought you were going to see and that you knew you needed to see vanishes, the light is wrong, the room is wrong, you are no longer sure who you know and who knows you, you quickly accept the terms of the new reality because that's what people do, but you never get over the feeling of serious, irreparable loss, a radio is clicked on in the dark, luxurious quiet of a fine automobile: crooners and white big bands, a continuous tide of litter sweeps up the street toward you, human beings, lit up by mercury and neon and halogen, gesture and loiter and stare, everything is cheap, tawdry, discounted and unbelievably expensive, magnificent old buildings rise up through the gloom and blight and advertising looking utterly ridiculous, deep thudding noises boom steadily around you, as if battleships a mile out on the lake are laying siege to the city, while citizens go desultorily about their midnight business, either secure in the belief that the fortress is impregnable, or simply unafraid of fire and sword, simply unafraid, having, perhaps, after all, nothing to lose . . . and we continued south on Halsted, jogged east then south into the Loop, drove aimlessly up and down empty streets, approached the Michigan Avenue bridge, the angels and heroes of *Regeneration* and *Defense* sculpted on the sides of the drawbridge pylons, crossed and saw in crossing the two Wrigley Buildings, the one brilliantly lit and seeming to move in the cloudy night sky, the other black and dim and bleeding away in the choppy water of the river, angels and heroes living in the former, the trolls responsible for all the misery and corruption of our glorious civilization in the latter, beneath the bridge, rising up like gas through cloaca and lead, a deeper insoluble poison rising up and spreading across the merely toxic current, collecting in backwaters, waiting for a hero to slip, to plunge from the good building to the bad, to drown there and to be reanimated by fallen angels with their oily halos, dripping tears of lead, ministering quietly in the burning sludge, patient in the darkening miasma, feverishly convinced of their rectitude in the disease they have made of the world, working to strip the drowned one of his principles, his compassion, his dignity and composure and spirit, then letting him wash up on the bank, to be found in an expensive suit and led back to the fairy tower, secure in the knowledge that money is everything.

We headed north, then circled around and angled southwest on Ogden, then south on Ashland, past an ancient sandstone fortress, the Church of the Epiphany, and Swanson babbled like a dilettante of architecture, or Willy Loman as a mob lawyer who really wanted to be an architect, calling my attention, with real joy, to the windows deep-set like a castle's, the Richardsonian Romanesque strangeness everywhere apparent, the intricately carved stones of the arches, the imposts, springers, voussoirs, extrados, intrados, keystones—all haunted, I thought, by the humble, careful hands that had done the work a century before. And Swanson said, "There's nothing left of the old neighborhood but I want to drive there and show it to you because I have a story to tell about it."

We drove south, the university on one hand, the hospital on the other, massive, fearsome, glowing buildings, institutions on which our civilization literally depends, the flags and banners of which hung limply from poles a hundred feet high, the air humming in the grid, the power audible even over the roar from the expressway and the Blue Line rails.

"At one point, midway through his career, after Cuba, Vegas, but before Hoffa, Frank saw himself, I say this to you confidentially, because I like you and I trust you and it's true anyway, saw himself as something like a Roman general. Mainly we were concerned at that time with prostitution and bookmaking day-to-day, and the wards and courts long-term, but he came to think of himself in that way. All I can tell you is that he did. One day he went around this very neighborhood—up and down these streets, anyway—and let it be known that he wanted the community, however they wanted to organize and administer themselves, to hand over one man to him for summary execution. He supplied no reason, no context. They understood that he did not need a reason or a context, and that if he had one, it was his business, not theirs. They understood that if they went about the problem in the right way, they would find the man Frank actually wanted. That is to say, they believed that there was a man who had somehow offended Frank, and that if they simply made his demand known, the guilty party would reveal himself. Frank told them that if he didn't have someone to execute in two weeks, to the hour, he would begin, at the beginning of the alphabet, to murder all the men in the neighborhood. Now what do you suppose happened?"

"I don't know," I said, dreamily.

"Guess."

"They found someone."

"Bingo."

"Did you—did Frank kill him?"

"What do you think?"

"I don't know."

"Guess."

"Yes."

"Bingo."

"Was he the guy Frank wanted?"

"What do you think?"

"I don't know."

"Guess."

"Yes."

Swanson made a sound like a game show buzzer. "YOU LOSE!" he shouted happily.

We drove.

"I had, we had, a little room, right over there, beneath what used to be a bar, that was my headquarters, and in this room I kept money. At the time of the Roman general, I had to wade through that room. Literally up to my armpits in cash. Had another room, same deal, only weapons. The only time I ever saw as much in the way of guns and money was down in Miami with Calero and those fund-raisers from what *was* it, the uh, the oh gee now what was it, the National Endowment for . . . I think . . . the Preservation of Liberty? And oh what was that other one! IDEA? What the hell could that have stood for?"

"Institution for Democracy—"

"Yes. Education and Assistance, that's right! Now how did you know that?"

"It was a day," I think I said, "when I didn't have my head up my ass."

"International Business Communications, that was the other one. All that contra crap, wow, we had to have a piece of that. But I'm way ahead of myself. You know what took us out of this quaint little district once and for all?"

"No."

"Guess."

"Can't."

"Jimmy Hoffa."

"Ah."

"Of course Jimmy had rooms full of cash, too! I suppose we all did . . . but those fund-raisers, boy, they really put me in mind of that first little room full of gold doubloons and diamond tiaras."

"Do you know who killed Hoffa?" (The reader will surely forgive me for what is implicit in the question.)

"I hated working for Hoffa, but I didn't do it. Frank hated him, too, but he didn't do it either. God, it was the worst part of our lives. He didn't like me, didn't trust me, wouldn't listen to what I had been told to tell him, very frustrating, very annoying. The last thing Frank ever did for him, and this is what sprung us from whores and gambling, he said, This is your last chance to see that I am your friend, you stupid fuck—Do you know anything about Hoffa? The infamous Test Fleet Case? In Nashville? He's got this guy standing guard at the door of his suite where all us lawyers are shrieking at each other and tearing our hair out, and it turns out that this guy, he flips and he's got evidence we were tampering with the jury, and Hoffa is indicted for that, goes down to Chattanooga, is convicted, goes to prison. Well, we know who actually was responsible and it wasn't the fellow at the door! Frank killed the guy who was, and Hoffa *never thanked him for it.*"

As you drive south, rounding the lake and heading for Gary, Chicago becomes more and more clearly the nightmare you suspected all along it was. The fairy dust settles as ash, the sweet perfumed fogs become acrid and something in them sticks to your skin, the hum of power becomes the hissing and snapping of cables fallen and writhing like beheaded snakes, vast fields of concrete and tall weeds open up suddenly and disappear at the horizon, roads go nowhere, immense vehicles, stripped and rusting, dot the plain like skeletons of buffalo, mastodons, woolly mammoths, dream animals, billboards advertise nothing but the inscrutable spray-painted answer to a question no one you know understands. Dead birds float in silver pools, locked gates prevent entry to places where nothing is, one or two wide-eyed people stare at a burning car, knowing their lives are now in real danger.

It comes at you in streamers and sudden bleak vistas, as if the ragged, tattered ends of a decaying but still lively Chicago were snapping in the wind and unraveling, and then disappears in the same way, as corn and bean fields subtly change the lines of the land and even the night colors, and stars become visible.

[23]

WE DROVE DOWN A LONG DIRT LANE toward a stand of dead windbreak trees, behind which were a collapsed barn and an old farmhouse. I could see no lights burning, but Swanson assured me Frank was inside. "He may be asleep," he said, in an almost fatherly way, fumbling with the keys, then opening the front door. "Frank, it's me," he called out. I could see nothing while he patted the walls for a light switch; just before he found it, I saw a thin line of light under a door.

The room was empty save a sofa. We walked toward the door under which I had seen light. "Frank, it's me," said Swanson, and opened the door.

Fini sat at a small table in an empty kitchen, gaunt, pale, eyes burning like a man dying of tuberculosis. On the table were an ashtray mounded high with butts, a bottle of vodka, and a tumbler full of ice. Fini dragged on his cigarette, looked at me in a way that was hard to interpret, either as if he hated me but was paralyzed and unable to do anything about it, or loved me and wanted me to help him. He nodded almost imperceptibly, reached for the bottle, and poured the tumbler full of vodka. Then he looked at the cupboard. Swanson went to the cupboard and brought two more tumblers and a bottle of bourbon to the table. We toasted each other with minute liftings and tiltings of our tumblers, and drank several rounds in silence. Then Swanson began to speak.

His theme, at first, was individualism. I had a hard time staying with him, for obvious reasons, compounded now by alcohol— but this is the one I wish I'd been wired for: sell it to David Mamet for a small fortune. What I thought he was saying was that Fini—and by extension, himself as well—was an individual, neither master nor servant, who accepted no authority of any kind beyond his own good judgment. He looked out for himself, and assumed other individuals were doing the same. Because the world was complex, he, of his own free will, entered into a union of like-minded individuals, and this group negotiated with other groups to secure their livelihood—pretty much the line I had tried and failed to use as an ice-breaker with Bernard Gummer.

Drinking heedlessly, I found myself getting rather passionately involved in the argument, and pointed out that his group produced nothing and was therefore preying on other groups, not negotiating with them. And I asked what was to prevent, in a world of ungoverned individuals, "a reign of universal rapacity and perpetual slaughter" (paraphrasing George Woodcock, whose primer on anarchism informed everything else I learned in college, and which I quote here), to which Swanson replied, "If a person or persons is not looking out for himself or themselves, I can't help him or them."

He drifted then from nineteenth-century egoism to ancient Chinese secrets, aphoristic remarks that sounded like half-baked *Tao Te Ching:* the ruler as shadowy presence, the people with their bellies full and minds empty, happy and ignorant, without will, knowledge, desire, the clever never daring to act, and so on.

"Frank feels he's wasted his life," Swanson said suddenly. "It's as simple as that, Jack. Flushed his essence, if you will, down crapper after crapper, let himself be charmed by superficial wealth and localized power, whore after whore."

I dared finally to look closely at Fini. He was smoking cigarette after cigarette, and had finished a quart of vodka, but had not said a word, had hardly moved. The vodka appeared to have softened not just his gaze—though something of a sneer on the lower lip remained—but his armature as well.

Swanson continued his monologue, speaking of their joint experience of savage and demented retired Air Force generals and slick can-do Marine colonels, multimillionaires who wanted only to have their pictures taken with President Reagan, a president who could and would take money for such performances, and glad-handed fund-raisers with clipped mustachios and taxpayer-supported money-laundering operations that made their mouths—Fini's and Swanson's—water, and that had finally suggested to them a new career, a new life.

Swanson said, "After a few years, Jackie boy, say as long as a decade, after every man, woman, and child in America has read our book—Frank's memoirs, edited by you, my commentary, edited by you, and your third-man, objective outsider's observations and criticisms—Frank comes out of hiding—and I'm not talking about federal witness relocation, we're hiding from them, too—Frank comes out of hiding and he runs for some goddamn elective office. We build up the organization, because organization is everything, am I right? Jack? Then, Christ, this government, this republic is resting on eggshells already. It would not at all be difficult for the right guys to set up a shadow government."

I was thoroughly drunk now, mercifully, and didn't blink. I slurred my words but I didn't blink. "Way's been paved. You wanna take over the government of the United States I'm telling you the way's been paved."

"Well, Jack, you're smiling so big, I hope that means you're enthusiastic and not, you know, making fun of us."

"Not makin' fun of you."

"Because, after all, I have seen Frank kill men for less."

"Couldn't be more serious!"

"I'm not talking about some kind of grandiose coup or revolution, you understand. I'm not talking about overnight. I'm only trying to suggest the outlines of what we see as *possible* and *what*, exactly, we have to lose."

This was probably the single greatest moment in my dealings with Fini and Swanson, when I saw how a pair of *almost* comically stupid, greedy, and violent men could, *conceivably*, subvert and eventually bring to ruin the democracy that ruled the world. The way *had* been paved: people like me (I don't mean me, I am clearly not the reporter I thought I was, might be, should have been) who might have blown whistles had been marginalized or demonized or, at best, forced into the motley of the Fool. The novelists, dramatists, and poets who might have disguised the truth as entertainments and fables all had their throats cut or their tongues ripped out and were focusing their talents on domestic dynamics, and not one citizen in a thousand had any idea of what actually happened when the events and episodes that constitute "Iran-contra" took place.

I looked out the window. A great funneling jet of a cloud appeared to be attached to the full moon. It looked like a billow of bright gas hissing from a leak in the moon. Slowly they separated, the triangular cloud, the circular moon, and Fini tipped his empty bottle of vodka over. Swanson got up to get another bottle from the freezer. Opening the freezer door, he stepped back suddenly, involuntarily, then collected himself and said, "What's this guy's head doing in here still?"

[24]

I WAS TOLD I COULD SLEEP ON THE SOFA in the living room. I lay down and Swanson sat on one of the armrests. He said, "You're right, these guys have wired the Constitution to explode. Could happen any day now. Just have to figure the angles. Jack?"

"Yeah."

"If I put a gun to your head and told you to kill someone, would you do it?"

"No," I said, without thinking.

"If I put a gun to your head and said take down your trousers and bend over, would you? Would you suck my dick with a gun to your head?"

"No," I said, fear suddenly gushing back up through the alcohol and the excitement (frankly) of being more or less kidnapped. It formed a pool, like oil, atop everything else.

Swanson sighed. "You're wrong. You'd do it all, trust me. Good night. Flying to Canada tomorrow. We'll do some fishing."

[25]

I AWOKE TO THE SOUND OF RAIN. It was loud on the old house and I listened to it for a long time. A small electric alarm clock showed seven when I first looked at it, and seven when I looked at it again, much later. I got up and made some coffee. A phone somewhere deep in the house rang and rang and rang and I had a chilling sense that it was me calling. After I realized the sound of the rain had diminished, I opened the front door. A blast of hot, wet air hit me. The rain felt like oil, my skin like butter, the ground quicksand. Of course I was hungover and wanted only to be left alone in some cold, dark place.

Fini and Swanson appeared on the far side of the collapsed barn. Swanson cupped his hands to his mouth: "You ready to go, sleepyhead?"

[26]

WE DROVE AROUND a medium-sized airport for what seemed like an inordinately long time, Swanson speaking in the clipped fashion of all pilots into his mike, smiling back at me regularly, reassuringly, me feeling like I was in a little rubber band-driven toy airplane. Then we picked up speed and suddenly were out over the lake. We went east, then banked sharply north and climbed steps of altitude as they were called out to us. Nobody spoke until Swanson gestured out his window. "Green Bay on our left, Door County Peninsula. An associate or two have summer homes down there. Very nice."

In the silver haze to the north lay Michigan's Upper Peninsula, and beyond it, Lake Superior. I had the fleeting impression we were flying toward a fairy kingdom, the splendid halls of the forest kings, cowled and antlered priests burning randomly chosen women, and then it somehow came to seem that it was the future that we were flying toward, that we had lifted out of time and were racing ahead of what we had done, what we could do, so as to perhaps spare ourselves the misery and horror of our deeds, of action, of consequence. The East was what? Where a person received orders from a master? And the North was where you went to report on what you'd done?

Relinquishing control to the autopilot mechanisms, Swanson turned in his seat and tried to explain violence to me. "Think of the market economy," he said loudly over the drone of the engines and the howling of the wind, "how it grows out of the market*place* economy. Do you know the difference between market and marketplace? I don't mean, let me say this carefully, the difference between a system—the market—and a zone or area of commerce—the marketplace. That's not what I'm talking about. Do you know what I mean?"

"No, I don't think I do," I shouted.

"Okay, economies used to be local and isolated in the, let's just say *in the past*, okay? Prices were set by custom, not by *what the market would bear*, which is the rule now. With me so far? We're talking about an alien world that is not capitalistic, nonentrepreneurial. The community regulates itself and its processes. A man could no more charge a higher price for a good or a service than he could hike up the skirts of his neighbor's wife. There was no basic understanding about *the right to make money*. I know, I know, it sounds absurd, but there's all kinds of statistics on this topic. These were the first Americans! New Englanders! Our forefathers, believe it or not, were not, strictly speaking, profit-oriented!

Freedom this and freedom that, yes, but it never occurred to them that they were free to make money! But times change, customs, populations—and when the prices for goods and services tend to converge, when the area of . . . when the geographical area of converging prices is broad, when more and more people participate in buying and selling, the market suddenly breaks free of all prior restraints, social, moral, what have you. Suddenly there are no brakes. Suddenly nobody cares that there are no brakes. Brakes are anathema! Everybody's a freewheeling entrepreneur and profit is everything. Suddenly *it's a right.* Suddenly it's what America is all about. Now here, Jack, is the leap: *it's the same goddamn pattern where violence is concerned.*"

[27]

SWANSON TALKED AND TALKED and talked. Some of it I remember well, most of it not at all. I remember a lull in which I got out my notebook—lost in the ensuing action—and made some notes. Swanson and, I assume, the silent Fini were inclined to see most people as idiots, and all idiots as enemies, because they had no sense of belonging with other people (other people belonged to them). I thought that that was what wickedness was, not putting a tin pot over somebody's head and beating it but seeing a great and important distinction between yourself and others. Goodness—and here I thought of Ricky Friend—came from making no such distinction, from seeing yourself as part of universal life. The irony of course is that Ricky wanted to kill himself, and Fini killed people who, more than anything, were mirrors of himself.

After a while, I stuffed my notebook back in my bag, and I asked Swanson if he was, or had ever been, afraid of dying. "I mean, say some idiot has an inspired moment and decides to deprive you of your life."

"Practically speaking, Jack, that's the first thing you get over. If you're afraid of dying, there's no place for you, you've got no business being alive. You're as good as dead! It's a basic trick. You find out what the other guy is most afraid of and nine times out of ten, it's dying! Just like that," he snapped his fingers, "you have the greatest advantage in the world. What, for instance, are you most afraid of?"

"I'm one of the nine. Dying."

"See? All I had to do was ask you and you gave me everything I need to know to destroy you. You're an idiot, Jack. I mean theoretically. You're my enemy."

I looked out over the wing at the silent shadows of clouds passing too swiftly, as if time were lapsing unnaturally for us, suddenly blackening a thousand, a hundred thousand acres as if with the plague, the swelling green of the forest canopy like nothing so much as a vast inland sea slick with rotting vegetation. The blinding lakes that broke into view and were instantly swallowed up were like blinking eyes, or white faces spotlit for a fraction of a second on a darkened stage—mirrors that did not reflect an image.

And Swanson said, "But I've employed idiots and enemies all my life. How could we avoid it, right, Frank?"

Fini said nothing. Swanson repeated his request for confirmation, and again Fini said nothing. Swanson seemed crushed. He was breathing heavily, as if fighting back sobs.

"Isn't that right, Frank? Frank? Frank? Frank, isn't that right?"

Fini said nothing, didn't move.

"FRANK, TALK TO ME! WHY WON'T YOU TALK TO ME? SAY SOMETHING! ANYTHING! WHY DON'T YOU JUMP OUT THE FUCKING DOOR IF YOU'RE SO MISERABLE?"

Fini said nothing. Swanson was breathing so stertorously, so painfully, it was worse than sobbing. I could hardly stand to hear it, and actually put my hands over my ears. Suddenly he threw the plane into a steep bank to the right, so that he was nearly on top of

Fini, whom he proceeded to stomp, as if trying to push him out the door, which was of course locked tight. But Swanson stomped as if his life depended on it.

After a while he stopped stomping and brought the plane back to level flight. Kicking halfheartedly and stepping crazily, like an angry child, he continued to hit at Fini, and then reached over and tried to open the door, but Fini lay too heavily in the way. Swanson was bawling now, tears streaming down his face, talking about the ten thousand in fees and how Frank should just kill him now, kill everybody, get it over with. But Fini merely rearranged himself in his seat and groaned.

After a few minutes more of droning flight, everything seemed to be better again. Swanson said to me cheerfully, "Blood thoughts without an enemy are sickening, they are nauseating physically, they are revolting. Blood thoughts with an enemy properly in mind are nourishing. When you neither have nor do not have an enemy, well then, that's when the going gets tough!"

[28]

SWANSON PICKED A LAKE from a thousand just like it, how I did not know and did not ask, and we dropped into it like a flat skipping stone, slamming into the water and roaring across the lake.

When we came to rest, we were on gently swelling waves in the middle of the lake. Swanson cut the engines and said, "Hand me the blue tackle box and the rod in the gray case? Thank you. This is kind of a ritual, Jack. First thing we do is fish from the plane. Just watch: got northern pike in this lake that'll practically jump into the cockpit."

The sun was beginning to set, the blues and greens blackening to the sky's red, and there was no sound save the click and whir of Swanson's rod and reel, my own increasingly labored breathing, and the sound of Fini groaning as he unscrewed the top of a bottle of vodka.

Then I heard a distant buzz and looked toward it. I saw something flash on shore, then made out a dock, a boat: they were, Swanson told me, Fini's Cree Indians, who looked after the place, firing up an outboard to see what might be wanted of them once the plane reached shore. He said, "This is such an isolated place." He was speaking tightly. "These people are so naive."

Fini groaned and sighed and drank, spilling vodka down his front. I closed my eyes and heard Swanson's rod and reel clatter against one of the pontoons. Then there was the deafening BOOM of a gun going off, and I opened my eyes to see Fini tumble out onto the pontoon and slip awkwardly into the water. There was blood all over the cockpit, all over me, all over Swanson.

The buzz of the outboard was louder now. Through the windshield I could see the bow of a little boat riding high in the water. Then the sound dropped off a little, the bow dropped, and I could see someone in the stern. Swanson reached under Fini's seat, found a small, flat pistol and tossed it to me.

"Okey-dokey," he said casually, "here's the deal. This is where I always said I wanted to die. 'If I can't live here, I'll die here!' You can kill me. Would you like to do that? Really be something to write about . . ."

"Kill you?" I whispered, "no."

"Well, darn it, you have to. Or I'll kill you. 'The highest pitch of every passion is always to will its own downfall.' Kierkegaard, Jack. Kierkegaard."

"Don't kill me, please," I squeaked.

"But I will!" shouted Swanson, as if trying to imitate a Shakespearean actor. "Now, Jack, come on, be honest, isn't this what you guys *really* want to know about us gangsters? Well, to *understand*, you must *do*. You live in your head too much, Jack. I know what that's like, believe me. But this is show business, the show must go on, you gotta kill me, this is your cue. Don't feel sorry for me, I've done very well for myself and my family. Do you know what happened to a dear friend of mine? Attorney for one of Frank's associates? He was having an argument with his boss, his client, and he said something like, 'You're crazy, there are too many details lying around, we've got to clean them up!' And his client grabbed a broom as if to sweep these details up, then busted the lawyer's teeth with it. Jammed it into his mouth and down his throat, and then, heaving with all his might, drove it down the length of this tall lawyer until it popped out his ass and the bristles were coming out his mouth like some crazy mustache. They taped a dustpan around his middle and hung him up in a janitor's closet. I, however, am going to *very slowly decompose* at the bottom of my beloved lake!"

I could see the man in the boat quite clearly now, and it was not a man, but a little boy.

"It's like those old Jew singers, Al Jolson and Sophie Tucker and Fanny Brice and whatsis—Cantor, Eddie Cantor. They put on blackface. My father used to love them. Said they blacked-up Tucker because she was too ugly otherwise. But they were really just in show biz, right? Couldn't be who they really were, because America wouldn't tolerate them that way. They wanted their entertainers just a certain way and no other. So they gave their audiences what they wanted and what the audience wanted was darkies with big white gaping mouths, animals, you see, who could sing. Did you know Jolson used to piss on people in public? When they bored him? Used to whip his pecker out and piss on 'em. Thought it was funny. I suppose it was! I mean, why not? Guy spends his whole life being someone else—but those were different times. My point is, if you can't be who you are, you be whoever you can be, whoever your audience will let you be. They couldn't be Jews so they put on blackface. See, this is George Swanson in mob face. Kill me or I'll kill the little Indian lad."

The outboard cut out and the boy drifted toward us on a swell of blue water. He was still far enough away—not wanting to disturb the fish with the motor—for me to think he was safe, but I could see that he was smiling.

"Don't, please don't kill a little boy."

"Fuck the little boy! We all die! What's the big deal!"

"Hey, Boss!" cried the little boy. He was already at the plane. His boat bounced lightly against a pontoon, making a watery *thunk.* Swanson turned toward his open door, his arm dropping like a drawbridge. The little boy belched a long, rolling belch, and laughed at himself. Then he saw the gun, said "Wow," and began, helplessly, silently, to cry.

[29]

I YANKED AMATEURISHLY ON THE TRIGGER and there was a big noise. Swanson tried to get on top of me, lunging and gargling in a very small space. Then he was on top of me, braying and fuming. Blood appeared, erupting from the unlikeliest sources. I spat it out, wrestled with the now stupendous weight of George Swanson, mob lawyer, millionaire many times over. There was another big noise, and my ears crackled. I felt a burning along my arm. Another noise, and another and another and another and another, muffled, or not so much muffled as remote. Swanson whinnied like a horse and died.

The extended Cree family nursed my tiny affliction and got me, literally, out of the woods. I wrote on a piece of paper toweling, *It's like a bad movie after all. I get the thrill of killing but don't have to pay a psychological price. I kill because I am saving a little boy's life, not to mention my own. But it's not true. There is always a price for such splendid luxury, such rare privilege.*

[30]

THERE WAS, PREDICTABLY, QUITE A LOT OF CASH in the luggage. Because I had none, I helped myself to it, giving some to the Crees, then heading south. Crossed the border in a rowboat, slept in a motel in Warroad, Minnesota—six dollars for the night—and took a bus to Saint Paul. There I had an excellent series of meals at the Saint Paul Grill, and lay awake all night, many nights in a row, in an excellent room in the Saint Paul Hotel, a fine old building across the street from Rice Park, where striking streetcar drivers once rioted. My plan was to remain incognito and incommunicado for as long as it took "to write a book." But I gave it up almost immediately and called Dorothy, who lived in a restored carriage house behind a mansion on Summit Avenue. She was properly horrified, but what, in the end, could she say?

"Consciousness is a very recent acquisition of nature, and it is still in an 'experimental' state. It is frail, menaced by specific dangers, and easily injured," she said, which wasn't bad, considering. It was a quote from Jung. Then she said she'd be happy to show the manuscript to her agent.

I went back to Chicago. Not a week later, I had cause to apply the Jung quote to thoughts of Ricky Friend, who made the news for two or three days. When I heard that he'd gone in for fancy Chinese breathing, I was cheered. It seemed like good news. He had found somebody who might be able to help him make sense of his life, of life, period. But the more I thought about it, the more it seemed to me to be something like what happened to the ex-Marine who was on the talk shows a while back, the son of the most decorated Marine in history, who had learned to walk the military walk and talk the military talk, bought it all, and more, believed it all, the moral frame for the polished boots and the shiny beribboned medals, who went to Vietnam proudly and got hurt badly, who came home in a wheelchair, disillusion growing like a thunderhead or cancer, until his life was a terrifying storm of drugs and alcohol and isolation, no walk of any kind, no talk at all. And then Recovery happened in the United States of America. He recovered. He cleaned up, sobered up, wrote a book about it. Walked the recovery walk and talked the recovery talk. Gave lectures and did talk shows. Then he killed himself.

The complete version of the Ricky Friend report includes the mention of what is in effect a suicide letter, addressed to "a Chicago newsman" who had disappeared and who was wanted by authorities for questioning regarding another disappearance. The letter is brief and reprinted in full: "At first I say this is a job but I look around and everybodys dead. Everybodys frozen up. I think who brought them here? I don't feel right about it. Was it me. I never felt good. Sometimes I felt good but whats the point. It must be me. I bring these good people here. It makes me feel like I am death. If I stop, it stops. Best wishes, Henrique Friend (from the morgue, man!)"

Somewhere along the line, perhaps through his Chinese adviser, or more likely on TV, he had come across the story of the Buddhist monk who incinerated himself in Vietnam, in protest of the war. I think Ricky thought he might make a similar protest. I think he thought that by setting fire to the cooler and to himself he might free a lot of souls, that in the sudden tremendous heat and concomitant "Disappearance of Death" (in the person of Ricky Friend), "numberless infinities of souls might arise and to their scattered bodies go."

[31]

WE MUST REMEMBER WE ARE TO DIE but overlong thoughts of death contaminate the soul like a plague the flesh. It is an abomination and the soul must be made clean again. It must be stripped bare and bathed in the fire of divine love. I am clearly quoting someone, as is my habit, but have lost the reference. But there is a flash of light when life can be seen for what it is and the flash of light is death. The dishonest man sees the flash and thinks in terms of evil and punishment. He schemes: I must live now, while I still can! He is overwhelmed by greed and fear and love and hope, the Grand Guignol cops-and-robbers boy-fucks-girl scenario that mad profiteers have reduced life and art to. The honest man knows it makes no difference what happens in the unbearably real world, and trembles, I think, as all he has known drifts uncertainly away from him: the money he has made and the taxes he has paid, the speeches he has made in defense of views he has held, the way his wife sometimes let her tongue slip between her lips when she concentrated on something she was reading . . .

I just now went outside, crossed the street to the high school, and saw the silver flagpole in the dark and littered yard. It was strangely bright in the gloom, as if possessed of a light of its own, not so much a bright light as one paradoxically dull and powerful at once. The pulley ropes tanged against it rhythmically, hypnotically. I walked toward it almost as if it were drawing me in. The closer I got the more it seemed to me the only object left in the world, the unbearably real world, the last pale, beyond which lay the greater universe. And I walked up to it, nearly into it, thinking I might conceivably *pass through it.* But I walked past on the left and it *snapped* out of my perception, almost audibly. It was gone as if it had never been.

How could Fini have become so powerless? Everything about his world (whose world?) suggested there were only two ways of being: powerful or dead. And yet there he was, the g-forces subsiding, Swanson sobbing at the controls: carefully rearranging himself in his seat, almost as if he'd simply sneezed, and not been stomped on by his lawyer—stomped on! Frank Fini! One of the most frightening and powerful men in Chicago! Everybody said so.

Perhaps the question is how could he not have become so powerless, having spent so much of it so ruthlessly and so quickly. No: *so carelessly.*

That's all I have to say about the United States of America. I've written the goddamn report and now I can give myself up. I can fall silent.

Peasants

"Ye are the salt of the earth:
but if the salt has lost its savour,
wherewith shall it be salted?
It is thenceforth good for nothing,
but to be cast out, and to be
   trodden under the foot of men."

Matthew 5:13

"When I waked in the morning, my first thought
would be, Oh, my wretched soul, what shall I do,
where shall I go? And when I laid down, would say,
I perhaps shall be in hell before morning."

Life and Journal of the Rev. Mr. Henry Alline

[1]

WHEN WALTER RASMUSSEN BECAME SO ILL that he could no longer ignore it, and believed he was going to die, he wanted to go home. He did not want to see his doctor, a man younger than himself improbably named Nutter who was as stern and clean-living as could be easily imagined and who would certainly ask questions about an above-average consumption of alcohol and troubled personal relationships that would be loaded with disappointment and disapproval if Rasmussen dared to defend himself. So he ruled out traditional medicine. He would not even get the blood work looked at. He would simply quit his job. If he was gravely ill, quitting his job would seem almost the only thing to do. Dying and broke, he would have no recourse but to go home. And yet it was possible he was not dying, he had to admit that, and admit as well that once it became clear he would have to go on living for some time, he would have to find another job—which would not be easy, as hundreds of thousands of workers across the country were just then being laid off, businesses were declaring bankruptcy, pension funds were being wiped out, the stock market tumbling, gas prices blowing through the roof of the economy and forming mushroom clouds. He had a good job with a privately held company that was performing anomalously well, even perhaps perversely, growing steadily, hiring, hiring, promoting, giving raises, maybe not *great* raises, but raises nevertheless, and adding—not subtracting—millions to the 401(k)s, expanding its business around the world and building new offices at home as quickly as the triggers of a hundred power nailers could be pulled.

Rasmussen was one of a select group of recipients, no more than two thousand, of this commercial wellness. He had in every way that could be enumerated and weighed a good job. And yet it was a cesspool, from which he felt he was crawling for his life.

Of course, it had, as the Buddhists are quick to point out, not always been so.

KYLE BOATMAN WAS Rasmussen's immediate superior. Born and raised in Perth, a boomtown on the west coast of Australia that had staggered when the boom was announced to be over, then fallen flat even as the last echoes faded into the desert outback, he had quickly become an American cowboy in his managerial style, combining the easygoing friendliness that was central to his character with a fast and loose entrepreneurialism that was proving decisive where his ambition was concerned. After just a year on the phone in Customer Service, he'd come up with a marketing idea that had caught the owner's eye: a series of books, lightly written, heavily produced, called How to Succeed in Geographic Information Systems Without Really Trying. Of course the "without really trying" part was ultimately rejected, but Boatman knew his boss liked musicals, and the lightheartedness of his presentation had been, he was later told, amusingly persuasive. Almost single-handedly he published the first book, *X Marks the Spot: GIS and Profit Maps,* then stood back and let the adulation wash over him: not only were the sales reps claiming they were clinching deals with the good-looking little books, they were actually selling them in bookstores. Boatman assembled a small team, came to terms with a canny small-press trade distributor, and put out half a dozen titles. When those titles exceeded expectations too, he was cleared to expand his team. He looked assiduously for independent thinkers, for creative people—and found them, roses all, proud of their thorns, a team that was looked upon with dismissive envy by the more traditionally organized, steeply hierarchical, and conservative groups around the company. Half of the team were men in their forties, half women in their twenties; the men affected comic avuncularity and discussed the women with secret, rueful admiration, to which the women responded with either frank but still somehow comic shows of disgust, or by showing off the straps of their underpants as they stretched about their offices and struck automobile-presenter poses around their computers. Or rather, by both. Sometimes the messages were confusingly, dangerously mixed, and sometimes the men found themselves embarrassed by latent alpha male tendencies they'd discovered in themselves.

"I darn't like to ply by the rules," Boatman had remarked with real seriousness and a strong Australian accent in the wake of a tour of the campus the company's founder and president had made and during which the team had been singled out for praise. "Whe's the fun in that? Ah like to do what's right, but Ah darnn't think Ah'm doing my job unless Ah'm reeskin' it." It went without saying that everybody on the team felt that way, too, and risked their jobs in their own unique ways. The workday was generally a satisfying and sometimes exciting one, as the unstable but powerful forces of sexuality were held in an uncertain but somehow orchestral equipoise mainly by the understanding that the best way to show off was to do good work: manipulate a skill over long hours, steer a project through stormy waters, come up with a brilliant idea or uphold a principle being neglected out of convenience, eat properly and get more exercise than was perhaps strictly speaking needed. Rasmussen dyed his eyebrows. He'd heard often enough that he was handsome for it to lurk as a definite possibility in the back of his mind, but his eyebrows were so pale as to be invisible. So he had his stylist darken them a shade or two.

A Golden Age ensued and lasted perhaps six or nine months. Then their society deteriorated and became corrupt. Two deep-minded and mysterious Russian men, big-picture theoreticians and analysts of almost meaninglessly obscure data, were based in another team but often found themselves on Boatman's turf, sometimes working up totally incomprehensible, even mad, book proposals or supplying completely inutile expertise, sometimes playing chess with one of Boatman's guys, Edward Cage, a poet and ethicist. Stukolka, the younger, had been one of the first to arrive at Chernobyl after the disaster, and Golubchek had been deported as a child during World War II to Kazakhstan. Their presence sometimes made the office seem like something out of nineteenth-century czarist bureaucracy, a militarized civil service organized by rank, and encouraged Rasmussen to imagine himself as a doctor in a Russian novel. That is to say, dashing, principled, doomed. *This is not intellectual work,* he vaguely recalled a character in a Chekhov story saying with disgust, *this is not honest work, hard manual labor is more honorable.* Three of the other men had worked for one of the region's bigger newspapers, and their presence lent an air of uncompromising, even ruthless, legitimacy to whatever happened to be going on. They spent a lot of time on the phone talking wholesale sense to people who needed to get a grip, and talked to each other for hours about the terrifying—not just terrible—consequences at the newspaper once the family who'd owned it had sold out to an international conglomerate. They winked at each other and at Rasmussen and whispered about how easy it was now, to make their evanescent duties seem crucial, and to appease Boatman with shows of mock-industriousness whenever doubt, anxiety, a weakening of self-confidence, or an obscurely guilty conscience gave the Boy Wonder pause, and brought on a round of meetings, or housecleaning, or requests for status reports, or the invocation, alternately solemn and sarcastic, of the name of the founder, Jack, who wanted something special done quickly.

One such suddenly exceptional project came about in response to an invitation to attend the World Summit on Sustainable Development, to be hosted by the United Nations in Johannesburg, South Africa.

In a state of nearly vaudevillian enthusiasm, Walter Rasmussen proposed a book that would link certain business opportunities in outer space and sustainable development practices on the ground, using geographic information systems (which was what the company made). The idea was considered with some faux rigor, but only briefly. Speaking for the group, Edward Cage demonstrated conclusively that whatever the project's merits were or might be, there was no time to do the thing well and should therefore not be done at this time. He was sick and tired of having to jump whenever the owner cracked his whip.

"If Jack wants a job done quick and dirty, he can crook a finger at Virtual Campus and they will be only too happy to oblige him. That is what they do. We on the other hand are here to help him resist the impulse for the quick and the dirty."

The ex-newspapermen rolled their eyes for each other's benefit, and one of the designers, a young woman from Indonesia who tempered her spicy exoticism with a keen appreciation of American scatological humor, suppressed a giggle with a hand placed mock-daintily over her mouth. "He said quick and dirty," she whispered to her friend, an even younger woman, the proofreader, who made a subtly comic moue. Rasmussen had gotten her job for her, because she had been a student, a star student, of his wife's (she taught romance and Chinese languages and literature) at the local college (considered a "high-desert Ivy"). He smiled knowingly across the table at her.

Cage, wittily observant when he wasn't speaking his mind, continued unimpeded. "We are here to *encourage Jack to see* that the kind of work he *really* wants done, does in fact get done. We are here to tell him when he doesn't know what kind of work that is. We are here to tell him he's flat wrong when he thinks he wants us to do some stupid job quickly and dirtily. We are here to do things well, and to make plain our judgment when a thing is so flawed at the outset that it can *never* be done well."

"No we're not," said Boatman, standing exactly on the line between an easy opportunity to make light of yet another of Cage's
attempts to argue Socratically toward individual enlightenment and
a deeper, clearer commitment on the part of the company to social
responsibility . . . and a wish to denounce Cage once and for all as a
tiresome fool. *"We're here to do what Jack asks us to do."*

Cage arose. He wore his hair long and his beard full because,
he said, that was what men looked like in nature. He also wore hand-
painted tennis shoes because mankind delighted in decoration. "Kyle
Boatman is a good man," he said. "And when a good man declares
we must do a thing, it behooves us, if we think we cannot do it, to
examine his motives. Why must we do what Jack asks us to do, Kyle?"

"Because he pays us."

"Does Jack believe, or act as if he believes, that we are
prostitutes?"

"Oh for Christ's sake will you sit down," begged Boatman, "and
shut up?"

Cage sat down as if his knees had given way, which caused
the titter he'd been hoping for, and threw his hands in the air. One
of the ex-newspapermen, Richard Gelb, speaking on behalf of the
young woman with whom he was secretly in love and who would be
tasked with design and production of the book, pointedly ignored,
with a subtle roll of his eyes, Cage's performance and declared it
was simply asking too much of an already overburdened but valiant
design and production crew to take on a book, the scope and dimen-
sions of which were unknown, with a deadline already in place that
would be daunting for even a completed manuscript.

The young designer for whom he had mounted his caparisoned
charger, usually reserved in group meetings and unironically cheerful elsewhere, surprised everybody by saying in a loud voice, "Amen
to *that*, Brother Rico!" causing the normally grim-faced and churlish
Gelb to ineffectually hide a smile and shift his weight around a sudden
tumescence.

"It's true," said Boatman, after everybody watched Gelb gulp for a few seconds. "I think sometimes we writers and iditors are a little bit in danger of taking our designers maybe a little bit too much for granted."

Rasmussen shrugged faintly and looked questioningly at his friends, the designers, but was met not with disingenuous battings of eyelashes, but with something rather more like indifference, or cool, level neutrality. *But how have I offended thee?* he mused for a moment. *I cannot think how.*

The newest member of the team, an older woman named Livia Barker—who'd been hired, it was rumored, by Boatman specifically to deflate the suspicion that he was capable of hiring only beautiful young women—spoke only for herself when she denounced the proposal as nearly indecipherable nonsense, smacking of incompetence and supportable only by the idea that Rasmussen's content providers were big shots. Because she had appeared deeply sedated during meetings concerned with her first project, and was feared, at least by Rasmussen, to be schizophrenic, this fierce rejection was interpreted as the belated staking of a claim and announcement of critical independence. Everyone looked askance at her, some a little startled, some a little amused, most just rocking slightly and reflexively forward from askance to bored. That she lived alone in the country—or rather not alone but with three ancient witches, two lionesses, and a python—served to weaken and magnify at once her reputation, situation, and prospects. No one knew, from one moment to the next, what to make of her, and her denunciation of the project had been so filled with barely suppressed fury that the idea was embarrassedly tabled. But Rasmussen, who often daydreamed of some kind of political career in which, from an office in Brussels or Prague, he would play a role in the making of international policy, saw himself shaking hands with Kofi Annan and thus inaugurating such a career, and took Boatman aside in the way Boatman liked to be taken aside. He assured him that not only could the project be accomplished in very little time, it would bring immense renown to the founder, the company, and the team as well.

Boatman was susceptible to that kind of vision. He took Rasmussen's toy spear down from the wall, where it rested on three pushpins, and poked Rasmussen in the belly with it. It was broken in half and held together with rubber bands, so the blade (rubber so withered it flapped when shaken) fell to the floor. Boatman continued to make poking gestures with the shaft, pretending the blade was still there, then making a face of comic dismay and saying "oh" when Rasmussen handed the blade back to him. Just as he finished fixing blade again to shaft, Edward Cage and Anita Portolan, the team's cartographer, stopped at the threshold of the sliding glass door and looked in. Boatman jabbed at them and shouted "Back to work!" Everybody laughed; the unpleasant tension of the meeting was behind them, and for a moment it seemed as if the playful high spirits of the old days had returned. Boatman was clearly in a mood to encourage such feelings, and swiftly granted approval of Rasmussen's project, which was what—he said—he'd intended to do in the meeting. It might have been preferable to have his vision affirmed in public, as it were, but this was a small, perhaps even mean, concern, in the face of a green light.

"You've got your work cut out for you, mate," he said, trying for a friendly but fatherly tone. "Darn't lit me dahn."

"I won't."

Everybody in the company, including the twelve directors who answered only to the owner, were paid, fascinatingly, by the hour, which meant that Rasmussen's take for the coming month would be substantially increased—very likely doubled and possibly even more— and Boatman alluded to this windfall as he stood to leave, making odd gestures with the spear, as if, Rasmussen guessed, he were some kind of primitive chieftain amassing great wealth. He looked up and down the hallway, then stepped back in. He leaned conspiratorially close and added that the long nights he was about to share with the designer wouldn't be so awfully hard to take either. Both men raised their eyebrows and smirked. Boatman then departed.

[2]

THE DESIGNER WAS ONE OF THREE WOMEN on the team named Jessica. The eldest, Jess Papantonio, was short and dark and Sicilian in her perceptions, predilections, and philosophy. The youngest, Jessie Wunderlich, was tall and blond, a spoiled brat from a wealthy family of doctors well known to and well liked by the owner and his family of Orange County orange growers. In the middle was Jessica Greenaway, a descendant of Okies and Arkies and men blown like tumbleweeds and debris into the mountains and deserts of San Bernardino County when the Orange County aerospace industry that had fetched them from the Confederacy imploded, was abandoned, and left to rust. On her office walls were photographs of the entertainer Jimmy Buffett and the stock-car racer Dale Earnhardt Jr., but she could easily have been working for the CIA for all she betrayed of her actual dark life in the course of perky cheerful comings and goings around the office. It was this last Jessica to whom Boatman referred. She had designed all ten of the books Rasmussen had written or edited, evidence accumulated in a very short while that they worked well together; and in fact their working habits and personalities were well suited to swift and inventive production: they enjoyed working together and were generally pleased with what they accomplished. Rasmussen was convinced his project could not be completed with another designer, and when he went to retrieve his spear (Boatman had walked off with it), he took a moment to make sure his boss understood his true feelings. Jessica, he admitted, certainly had the long shapely legs of a dancer, a fresh girl-next-door prettiness, hair right out of a shampoo commercial, and remarkably large breasts, but lustful thoughts had not entered his conscious mind. It seemed far more valuable that they could help each other pass the working day amiably and effectively.

"I was only kiddin' yer," said Boatman gently.

"I know," smiled Rasmussen. It was possible they had actually become friends: that kind of sympathetic warmth was certainly in the air.

"I know yer havin' a hard time," said Boatman. "I shouldn't be so rough with yer. *Not to mintion—*" he chuckled, *"being such a bloody pig about women in the affice!"*

Rasmussen waved the concern aside. "It's just between you and me. We're men. We're assholes. We can be frank with each other."

"Too right we can," said Boatman with real feeling. "And the truth is, I'm crazy about my wife." Rasmussen already knew, because they had been counted, recounted by various small groups, and gossiped heavily about, that there were twelve photographs of Boatman's wife—an actress who was admittedly quite pretty—in frames or tacked up everywhere you looked: from the glamorous head shot to silly birthday poses and family groups, old pictures from as far back as grade school, new snapshots taken the day before. He glanced at the ones nearest him—some kind of fancy, celebratory meal at a restaurant—said that, yes, that was great, and excused himself.

Back in his own office, however, Rasmussen paused in midthought, suddenly unsure how his boss had come to believe he was having a hard time. They'd had no heart to heart talks, certainly; perhaps it was the product of a series of knowing looks and suggestive facial expressions and gossip. It was somewhat troubling to think of the provenance, but that Boatman should sympathetically "know" something about Rasmussen's life was not actually disturbing, so he set the concern aside and briskly drew up a schedule whereby a small book of enduring value would be ready for shipping in two months. Then he called his wife. Their long marriage of riches and poverty, sickness and health was in a terrible state, near collapse.

That very morning she had watched him intently as he raced to get out of her sight and declared just as he was about to, that he had sailed past her understanding. And that was how it was: she evidently had some specific complaints, but he had somehow simply lost the desire to be in the same room. Then it had become a positive mania to get out of the room. Sailed past her understanding. His own, too, if that had anything to do with it.

When she answered the phone, he was filled with sadness and regret. "Returning to port," he said hopefully.

There was a long and sigh-filled pause. "Whatever you say, matey."

Rasmussen hung up the phone and stared at it disappointedly, as if the fault, whatever it was, lay deep in the technology, and not in his heart, which was on his sleeve and obviously not in great shape but still at the end of the day a heart.

On his way to the coffeemaker, he ran into Jess, who seemed to be a real friend. She seemed to understand, where he could not, the nature of the sins he was committing, and forgive them, as he could not even if he understood, even as she watched his marriage to a woman she also considered a friend die slowly of poison. But she was leaving. She was threatening to leave, anyway, to give notice and move to San Francisco, where her brother lived and where, she said, she would not have to have her teeth cleaned and repaired by Republican harridans. *They strap you down and get all their weapons in your mouth so you're afraid to even blink and then they say things like I am so glad those Minutemen are down on the border standing up to those horrible Mexicans!* She had wanted to move for years, but it had taken an insulting performance review to sufficiently disgust her and begin to give voice to that disgust: after a year spent compiling a dictionary of geographic information systems terms, she'd gone into the review, with Boatman's boss, expecting a raise, but had gotten nothing instead. Boatman refused to go to bat for her, explaining that his boss felt she could have used

an intern to compile the dictionary. He was sorry, he certainly believed no such thing, he thought he had a SWAT team, not a bunch
of rent-a-cops, but what could he do?

Rasmussen poured her a cup of coffee and asked her what had
gotten into Jessica the designer at the meeting that morning.

" 'Amen'?" he asked. " 'Brother Rico'?"

Jess's hair was very short, but she pretended to shake out a
luxurious mane, then leaned forward and pressed her breasts together. "Giggle giggle giggle!" she said, then stood up. "Too much
liqueur in the coffee today."

"Liqueur?" asked Rasmussen. "Really?"

"Bottom right desk drawer," Jess confirmed. "Fucking liquor
store in there."

Rasmussen laughed. "Really?"

"Giggle," said Jess. "Giggle giggle fucking *giggle*. It's like working in a fucking beer commercial."

The next day Boatman appeared silently over his shoulder, like
death, and like death, again, but this time on a pitcher's mound, threw
him a curve.

"Split the project with Livia."

"What a dismaying thing for you to say."

"Come on, man."

"I wouldn't split this with anybody, much less fucking Livia."

"*Hey*," said Boatman sharply. "You thought she was great
when we were interviewing her!"

"*Hey*," said Rasmussen, "*I was wrong.*"

"You haven't given her a chance, man."

"It's *my* project, Kyle! I thought it up all by myself!"

"It's the *team's* project, Walt."

"Too many cooks in the kitchen."

"Find something for her to do."

Rasmussen was already overexcited. "SHE WILL ONLY SLOW
ME DOWN."

"She needs to see how our process works, man."

"I'm not even sure why we're wasting time talking about it."

"And you need to stop shouting at me, dude!"

Rasmussen closed his eyes and clenched his teeth. Then he opened his eyes, exhaled, and loosened his jaw. "I'm sorry," he said.

"I am your boss, you know."

"I know it. I'm sorry."

"You've got to watch your temper," Boatman said quietly but with a bright red face. "I don't want it to become an issue here. It's a serious liability and you have a real problem controlling it."

"You're right," said Rasmussen, ashamed of himself. "You're right and I'm sorry."

A big and important chapter in one of Rasmussen's books, more or less its centerpiece, on which a great deal of time and money had been spent (he'd flown to Hawaii, for one thing), had been excised in the eleventh hour due to loss, Rasmussen liked to say, of cabin pressure. It was a book on disaster planning and response, and he'd worked up a great piece of journalism describing the methods, practices, and technologies of the Pacific Disaster Center, only to learn that the PDC was run by the Pentagon and that the Pentagon would have to approve the chapter before they would allow publication. The man at the Pentagon turned out to be, in Rasmussen's estimation, a supercilious nitwit who insisted on changes to the text that had nothing whatsoever to do with facts or substance, changes Rasmussen in turn insisted were his concern, not the Pentagon's. Approval nevertheless was withheld, pending a satisfactory revision of the text.

"I'm not making those changes," Rasmussen declared.

"Then you won't get my approval," said the nitwit. "I'm afraid it's as simple as that."

"No," said Rasmussen, "tell you what. I'll CUT THE CHAPTER FROM THE BOOK." In the buzzy silence that ensued, Rasmussen asked if that was in fact not even simpler.

"Do it as a favor to me, man," said Boatman.

"All right, all right, you win," said Rasmussen.

Livia Barker's office was lit only with a single desk lamp, and decorated with astrological charts and symbols, a large and heavy stone Buddha, and several framed photographs of her animals, one of which showed her nuzzling one of the lions and smiling with such radiant joy that it was impossible not to feel a little joy one-self. Rasmussen felt a surge of respect and admiration for her; she was perhaps more lonely than crazy, clearly capable when the full resources of her deep character were available to her, no matter how easily and unpredictably she might collapse in dither or bluster or apparent catatonia. That she preferred the company of the non-human to the human was evidence of good, not deranged, sense. Rasmussen smiled the smile he believed to be his most engaging.

For her part, Livia loathed Rasmussen and would have made no bones about it had she been able to find and use adequate means of expression. It was a personality clash of the first magnitude, and she found herself unable to do it justice except by accident. These accidents occurred frequently, but because they were accidents they were unsatisfactory.

It had not always been so. She had once, in the early going, confessed to Jessica that she thought Rasmussen looked like a movie star. Jessica had elbowed him sharply and simpered, "She *likes* you!" Rasmussen had made a face, rolled his eyes, shook his head vigorously, but later, privately, could find no objection in himself to being likened to a movie star. He began to think that charm might be the essential element in all dealings—and perhaps not solely with Livia Barker. But it had proved, in a very short while, an ineffective strategy.

Hearing him tap on the glass of her door—all of their offices had glass walls and sliding doors on the corridor—she swiveled in her chair and regarded him silently for a moment, as if she were a forgotten movie star or a very wealthy woman who'd cultivated reclusivity all her life. In her smile Rasmussen saw not the faintest trace of radiant joy.

"Kyle said you'd be needing some help," said Livia. "He thinks you may have bitten off a little more than you can chew." And here she laughed, as if to suggest they were comrades after all, and there was a flash, quickly darkened, of radiant joy. "I understand we'll all get to go to *Africa* for the summit." This was the least, it turned out, of what Rasmussen hadn't heard, of what his boss had said to other people about him, but he said nothing, squaring the edges of her copy of the project plan and reaching out toward her with it. A steaminess had arisen in Livia's veiled and joyless eyes and Rasmussen was afraid she was going to start playing with herself (a practice, according to office gossip, that she alluded to either subtly or coyly or with frank bawdiness in the offices of the other women in the group). But when he gave up trying to hand the papers to her and placed them on her desk, she seemed to lose focus, or hope, and looked away uncertainly. Rasmussen was so uneasy he banged into the glass door on his way out.

THE PROJECT DID NOT GO WELL. Rasmussen asked Livia to draft an introduction to the impact GIS could have on world peace, while he concentrated on health, wealth, and wisdom, but she had fallen into a state of unshakable torpor and had presented him only with a list of Web sites.

"I'll do it myself."

"Kyle told me this was good."

"Kyle told you this was good."

"Yes," insisted Livia. "He did."

"I don't know what I object to more, you going to Kyle with this before you brought it to me, or you going to Kyle period."

"Why shouldn't I go to Kyle?" she whined.

"What are you, some little schoolgirl bringing your homework to your teacher?"

"Kyle is my boss," she said, strangely like a little schoolgirl.

"Kyle is not the boss of this project."

"I'm afraid he is." Now she was arch and condescending.

"I am the boss of this project, Livia."

"Boss!" she squealed. "Don't make me laugh!"

"I'll do more than make you laugh."

"We are co-editors of the project. Reporting to Kyle."

"No," said Rasmussen simply. "We are not."

"Kyle also told me you were having emotional difficulties and that I should cut you some slack."

Rasmussen leapt from his chair so violently that it rolled backward and slammed into his desk, actually bouncing up a little off its wheels. Trembling, he inserted himself in Boatman's office and demanded to know on what grounds Boatman thought he could discuss the personal life of one team member with another.

"I nivuh sid that," said Boatman.

"Oh, she made it all up then, did she?"

"You know her, man."

"Of course I know her! That's why I said I didn't want her on the project! Jesus Christ! Now I'm supposed to *know her* when just yesterday I had her all wrong!"

"That's about right, yis," said Boatman.

"I'm too busy for this horseshit."

"It's not only company policy that such discussions are inappropriate, it's my personal belief as well. I don't want to bring our home lives to work. But speaking as your friend, I think you need to watch yourself."

"What are you talking about now?"

"You know exactly what I'm talking about."

Neither man, as it turned out, knew exactly what he was talking about. But the violent turn that the conversation had taken did not seem inappropriate. The question of knowledge, of who knew what about whom, and why it mattered, had leapt into another dimension of meaning and importance and consequence. The violence was the natural product of the men drawing nearer a truth, the actual revelation of which would not occur until some unknown date in the future, but which both sensed, dimly and inarticulately, but unmistakably.

A few days later, Livia Barker was quietly shifted away from Rasmussen's project, but they were sailing into darker waters. If Rasmussen was in Jessica's office for longer than an hour, he could depend on her taking a call from her husband; if they were in his office, he could depend on her taking the call on her cell phone. She had gotten married only a few months earlier, but the young and lively designer's cool reception of these calls could in no way be understood as part of ordinary honeymoon insufferability. She began to favor Rasmussen with looks of comic weariness, raising her carefully plucked eyebrows over the phone held close to her cheek. Then she took to groaning whenever the phone rang. Finally she made the nastily derisive *yak yak yak* motion, flapping fingers and thumb, and Rasmussen had to ask what was going on.

"He's a very jealous person," Jessica said.

"Ah," said Rasmussen. "That's too bad."

"He bought me the cell phone as a present even though he knows I don't like them. And when I leave it at home, he pouts and says I must not like presents very much and he'll remember that next time he thinks he might buy me something. He used to pout, anyway. Now he more or less insists I keep it near me at all times. If he calls and I don't answer, he gets nervous and starts calling every few minutes. If too much time goes by, he gets hysterical. I don't mean he gets mean, or crazy: he gets frantic and almost starts to cry."

"Ah," said Rasmussen, terribly embarrassed.

"That's how it is."

"I'm sorry to hear that."

"It's okay. I'm not a whiner." Jessica stretched her long legs out, then put her feet up on the corner of his desk. A period of silence ensued, in which Rasmussen became aware of a very delicate fragrance in the air, studied the legs angling up from one side of his tiny office to the other, and had to admit that while he found jealousy a preposterous evil in his fellow men, and consequently sympathized with Jessica—perhaps even feared for her safety, as there was no telling where unchecked jealousy might lead a man—he nevertheless had seen patterns of seductively subtle flirtatiousness in nearly every mode of her behavior, in nearly every environment and situation, cognizance of which troubled him even more deeply, as it amounted to him thinking *she's asking for it.* Backing sharply away from such a thought, he made a joke about how all the men in the office had grumbled when she got married: *He better treat her right or he'll have us to answer to!*

"That's all I need," said Jessica with a straight face. "More uncles."

They were on the third floor of one the newest buildings on the campus and went out onto one of its many balconies. The jacaranda trees that dominated the landscaping were in full bloom, and so they seemed almost, if they narrowed their eyes, to be adrift in a purple sea, beyond which the mountains sparkled, not yet obscured by the hot, thick, choking smog of summer. An electrical contractor's truck drove by, passing from purple cloud to purple cloud. The truck appeared to slow somewhat, and the driver to peer up at them; it was too far away to tell. Jessica watched the truck until it was out of sight.

"That was Travis," she said. Then started a countdown. "Ten, nine, eight, seven, six—" and her cell phone rang.

[3]

JACK THE FOUNDER'S ENTHUSIASM for his company's participation in the World Summit on Sustainable Development waned to the point where the existence of Rasmussen's book surprised him when it was finished and presented to him. "'Right, right . . .'" Boatman reported Jack as saying while he was flipping through it.

"'Right . . .'" Rasmussen had sighed and said he guessed that meant they weren't going to Jo-burg. "Well," said Boatman sheepishly, "*you* won't, and I'm sorry as hell about that. But there's a chance I'll go. Jack and I. I hope you're all right with that." Rasmussen blinked heavily and slowly, blood surging through all the wrong places in his brain, then nodded as if his head weighed a hundred pounds.

Out on the balcony, Edward Cage laced his fingers together in a church and steeple, then pressed the steeple to his lips. "That's Kyle Boatman all over. We can't expect otherwise from him. Shouldn't, any road. He's a feckless opportunist and that's all there is to it."

An astonishing number of people from the team were seated around one of the balcony's little tables. Some kind of board game was being, or had recently been, played, and it was still more or less lunchtime, but the true nature of the meeting was seditious. It had begun simply and innocently as a coffee break during which Anita Portolan, the cartographer, and Satyavati Swenson, the Indonesian graphic designer, compared notes over the countless meetings they were being forced to sit through as participants in a very large and in-contestably important project, an atlas of the Salton Sea, in which the company's partners were various state agencies and a local university. They cultivated a blossoming friendship, as well, and the meeting swiftly became a clearinghouse for workday complaints voiced with increasing frequency and incredulity and eventually even bitterness. It was explicitly understood that workers in even the most idealistically principled and benevolently administered companies complained, that complaint was ordinary and necessary and not to be taken either too seriously or not seriously enough . . . but something had happened in the course of these impromptu meetings, and their character had changed markedly. Something was going wrong in the group; it felt increasingly wrong and bad, but no one could say precisely what was wrong or bad, try hard as they might. Part of the problem, it seemed, the one outstanding feature in the murky scenario, was that some people knew some things, and some others did not know those things, those people in turn knowing other, usually contradictory or hostile, things, some knowing some things some of the time but not all of the time, others knowing a little of everything all the time but not enough to make understandings cohere—and consequently, a growing sense of unease that became less articulable the greater, and thus more obfuscating, the feeling became. People misjudged what they knew, or were simply afraid of it, sorry they knew, but determined to find a way to make it work for them. *You have sailed,* Rasmussen thought, *beyond my understanding.*

Because he had heard passionately vicious denunciations of team members who were not part of the circle, Rasmussen always entered the balcony scenes as if he were at a party where he could see no one he knew. He was not at all sure if he was part of the circle, and was not entirely comfortable with plots against the life of Boatman, whom he was, almost against his will, coming to think of as a friend, despite obvious differences of temperament and occasional clashes of vision. And yet, his co-workers around the table seemed to welcome him, seemed delighted, actually, that he was joining them, even to hang on the words of his witty commentary. He therefore wished to speak amusingly but moderately of their travail, to denounce Boatman with one ironic breath and defend him with another, more sincere, and did so at first, but found himself slipping, with incredible ease and facility, into a kind of sleazy comedian's nightclub routine, full of careless vitriol on one hand, and show-stoppingly inventive slander on the other. It had occurred to him that the tone was terribly similar to the only one he seemed able to employ in discussions with his wife. There was no understanding what that said about his character.

Some days, of course, were more lighthearted than others, and this day was clearly one of manic high spirits.

"Any *road?*" asked Satyavati. "What the fuck does that mean?"

"Means the same thing as any *way,*" said Cage.

"Ohhhhhh," said Satyavati. "I get it. You being creative!"

"It's dialect," said Cage. "A regional variation."

"How come nobody else says it? Must be a different region, huh? You come from some far-out other region, huh man?"

"No," Cage admitted, "I come from here."

"Okay, why you talk like you from some other region then, huh man?" Satyavati's English was excellent, but she liked to put on a show, like she was just off the boat and hustling. "Your other region is full of bullshit, man. I have to kick your ass, you come from some other region."

Cage laughed. Then he stood and walked to a corner of the balcony, pretending he was a bad little boy or the class dunce. He sulked, but how much of this was pretense was a good question. He much preferred humiliation at the hands of a pretty woman to making a point, elucidating a mystery, or winning an argument, but would manage the latter three over the course of the next few days, flooding the young Indonesian's e-mail in-box with defensive information. To which the young Indonesian would inevitably reply, "Why you gotta send me so much bullshit all the time, huh man? What I need this information for anyway?"

"Any road."

"I kick your dialect's ass, man."

Everybody laughed and when they were done laughing, Rasmussen told them that the Johannesburg junket was off, but that Boatman likely would get to go.

"*Motherfucker!*" bellowed the tiny Satyavati. This seemed to point directly at the nevertheless still obscure source of wrongness and badness. "I kick his ass too!"

Even though her name derived from Hindu myth, and her family was devoutly Muslim, Satyavati was a Buddhist, and as they walked back to their offices, she and Rasmussen talked about suffering.

"Are you happy?" she asked. Though it was more or less rhetorical, Rasmussen said that he was not. "Why not," said Satyavati.

Rasmussen shrugged. "Because you want all this shit, dude. If you didn't want all that shit, you would cease to suffer."

"Well, sure, I guess I understand that. I mean, it makes sense, and theoretically, I think it's a good idea, but . . ."

"If you stop wanting all that shit, it's easier to think kind thoughts about other people, and if you think kind thoughts, you do kind actions. That's good karma, dude. It follows like the wheel of the cart follows the hoof of the ox that's pulling it. Makes the world go round."

The wheel was indeed turning, and the shadows of the cart and the ox were moving toward them, but despite that it was an entirely appealing philosophy, and Rasmussen promised Satyavati he would consider it. He actually had a copy of the *I Ching* in his office, and three pennies in place of the fistful of yarrow stalks, but this seemed not quite the same thing. Valuable, certainly, and many of the oracle's judgments called for a similar kind of common sense—persevere in good undertakings, stop persevering in bad undertakings—but where he was always asking the oracle to solve a problem or console him with hints of good fortune, Sati's basic Buddhism urged him to stop taking himself so seriously, to give up on all the little characters he peopled his ridiculous stage with, and who, he feared, had all but driven him mad with their anarchic upstaging of each other, crying *you are so extraordinary, save yourself, save yourself, escape!*

He sat in his office, swiveling in his chair and jingling the pennies in the palm of his hand. If he swiveled far enough to the right, he could just see Sati's office, decorated with tastefully vivid and usually hilarious graphic designs, her pet frog in his tank, the flowers, the cartoon action figures, the prayer flags, and he wished, he yearned most ardently, for a better character. Not only had Sati suffered the terror of the Indonesian withdrawal from East Timor, not only had she been mother to seven younger brothers and sisters, not only had she traveled halfway around the world to start a new life in a strange land, not only had she put herself through college, but her husband was ill, very ill. Rasmussen didn't know any details, but he knew it was cancer and just the thought of it alone made him afraid. As miserable as he was in his marriage, he could not imagine his wife that sick. Could not imagine her dying. He thought, plunging into a sentimentality he would find embarrassing in anybody else, he thought that he would do anything to prevent such misfortune. And yet there was Sati, cheerful and at ease. The thought of escape would have made her laugh, he thought. *Why I want to escape, man? I kick escape's ass!* He could hear her saying it and he smiled, jingled the pennies, swiveled in his chair. Her participation in nasty rounds of gossip didn't fit the little hagiography he had daydreamed, but that seemed merely an ordinary flaw in a deeply good person.

One of the former newspaper reporters, a small, neat, balding man named Robert McElroy, walked by and grinned at him. It wasn't manly, either, gossiping around a table, clucking and braying. McElroy's quiet dignity always encouraged Rasmussen toward quieter dignity himself, and he got up to follow McElroy into his office for a chat about violence and drinking. One of their conversational chestnuts was the prediction of the only future either of them could honestly hope for, and that was living in a downtown flophouse and drinking themselves to death. "Just lining the bottles up on the windowsill," said McElroy. "Listening to scratchy old 45s on one of those sturdy schoolroom record players. Muddy Waters. The Yardbirds. 'I'm a Man.'"

Nor would the rigorously exemplary Jess Papantonio be caught dead even observing such a spectacle of capitulation to stereotype and "approved behaviors" as office gossip. Rasmussen stood in her doorway now, watching her swivel in her chair. He still had the pennies in his hand, and was flipping them up in the air rather than jingling them.

"If you bring a problem to the attention of your commanding officer," she said, "in an intelligent, principled, and constructive way, you will instantly be identified as a troublemaker and permanently sidelined." She stood suddenly, saluted, and shouted: "SIR! YES, SIR!" and sat down again, swiveling excitedly. "If you sit and bitch about it for hours a day instead of doing your job, you get a fucking *raise*. If Kyle doesn't see you as a father figure or a little sister or, or, I don't know, a daughter, *some kind of dependent woman, you are fucked.*" She put a hand over her mouth and suppressed laughter that was bubbling out of her. "Did I just stand up and shout *Sir! Yes, sir?*"

"I believe you did," said Rasmussen. He leaned backward and peered up and down the hallway. "It has gone unremarked."

"I'm TRYING to get some SLEEP in here," said Edward Cage, two doors down. "If you DON'T MIND?"

"He probably actually *is*," said Jess.

"Or playing FreeCell or—"

"Last time I looked, he was writing a letter to *el presidente*."

Because the company still thought of itself as small and freewheeling (the phone directory listed two thousand employees by first name), and because Cage insisted that the president of a small freewheeling company would welcome the concerns of the people he was urging to wheel freely, he regularly wrote letters to Jack the founder, taking him to task for various corporate offenses. These were very like the letters to the editor that Cage wrote to newspapers and magazines, and other, larger corporations, like General Motors and the federal government. He was particularly fierce with the local classical music radio station, which he found willfully ignorant, even contemptuous, of twentieth-century music. Rasmussen, who had grown up listening to the Animals and the Yardbirds and Cream, and who had spent his high school years solemnly but soulfully holding aloft large cans of beer as the Lynyrd Skynyrd anthem "Freebird" worked itself up into a passionate frenzy, now imagined he preferred the baroque, and he and Cage would argue happily about it for hours, Rasmussen wondering why Cage wasn't satisfied with tests of the emergency broadcast system and static or the jackhammers and dump trucks outside their offices, Cage allowing that while Bach was a decent composer, he was not as important historically as Cage's namesake, John Cage, would soon be seen to be. Telemann and Buxtehude excited only a most cordial loathing. As if to renew the argument, Cage now put a CD in his computer and turned the volume up, so that the entire hallway could hear a woman screaming for nearly thirty seconds. Then he ambled over to Jess's doorway and put his arm around Rasmussen.

"I would take even the four minutes and however many seconds of silence to that," said Rasmussen.

"Those four minutes and thirty-three seconds were anything but silent," said Cage.

"*Yes, yes, yes,*" sighed Rasmussen. "*I get it.*"

"I can hear him laughing right now," chuckled Cage. "He had a wonderful laugh."

"You're not related to him, are you?" asked Jess.

"No, but I did pluh—"

"*He did play several games of chess with him,*" Rasmussen interrupted. "That's why he can share that laugh with us right now. Which strikes me as suspiciously condescending. If John Cage were to laugh in a tone similar to the tone you are using right now at my failure to like his four minutes of—"

"He wasn't in the least condescending."

"He'd fucking well better not be," said Rasmussen with mock-truculence that was perhaps more persuasive than it needed to be. "Better not *have been,* I mean." He was now meek. "May he rest in peace."

Kyle Boatman approached Jess, Cage, and Rasmussen in his genial way, and was easily included in the banter, even when the subjects were potentially flammable, even explosive, even when he was the target of carefully calculated derision. And Rasmussen covertly studied his boss. He felt guilty, there was no question about that. A little voice, coming from one of the less talented

GARY AMDAHL

characters on his psychological stage, whispered that the problem was perhaps more accurately, more helpfully, to be located
within Rasmussen himself, but this met only with what Rasmussen
couldn't help but think of as a chorus of disapproval. The idea
was roundly booed by actors, audience members, and stagehands
determined that Rasmussen should lead a life of special elevation
and charm. Still, he walked and joked with Boatman back to his
office, where Boatman stopped him, then slid the glass door shut.
He then told him he had fixed it so that the two of them would
share a room at the big annual conference coming up the next
month. Normally roommates were paired randomly, but Boatman
was planning on having a guest in their room, an uninvited and
nonpaying guest who would be in a sleeping bag on the floor, but
one whom Boatman was sure Rasmussen would be happy to meet,
a man who personified the maverick entrepreneur, *a bona fide*,
insisted Boatman, *genius*.

"You don't think," asked Boatman with an air of chummy
winking confidentiality, "that I intind to stay here all my life, do you?
Doing *this*? Do you?"

[4]

THE CONFERENCE WAS THE MOST IMPORTANT EVENT of the
year for the company. It was called a "user's conference," and was
designed to put people who were using the company's software
in innovative ways in casual and collegial but exciting and intense contact with the software's masterminds. It took place in
San Diego, with half the company in hotel rooms and the other
half busing back and forth every day from headquarters, two hours
away—coffee breaks alone, they were warned, cost forty thousand
dollars. Almost no one in the entire company of two thousand put
in an ordinary day of nonconference work, and if it was a long,

102

exhausting, often drearily boring exercise for many employees, it was an ideal environment for a networker like Kyle Boatman. Rasmussen felt sluggishly adrift in the great flow, easily caught in backwaters, but found it pleasant to be out of the office, and away from home. Though the atmosphere was markedly, pointedly of born-again true believing in the world-changing potentialities of the software, rather than hard drinking and adultery, he drank hard and flirted with a kind of abandon that was amusing at first but that steadily deflated his spirits. The third Jessica, Jessie Wunderlich, who had been fighting off suitors for hours and looked like she might start slapping some of them, told him his deep stare was becoming more and more opaque until finally she thought he looked faintly cross-eyed and more than a little menacing and said he should knock it off. Then someone said something about a foreign country and she told the story of a friend of hers who had lived in that country, and the father of that friend, who was dying but who swore repeatedly that he would not die until he had seen Jessie naked.

"He was soooo sweeeeet," she said conclusively. Then she leaned into Rasmussen and whispered in his ear that the menacing look was actually kind of special, kind of intriguing, and that none of the other losers in the bar who were clamoring for a similar treat before dying would be able to muster such a stare until the third or fourth date. Her lips were brushing his ear and she said he could take that up to his room, to, so to speak, his little piggy bank.

THE ROOM WAS ON THE TWENTY-SEVENTH FLOOR, and offered a compelling view of the harbor. All day long dreamy images of imperial force drifted under and over and beyond the magnificent white arch of the Coronado Bridge: battleships and aircraft carriers, helicopters, jet fighters, all moving so silently and slowly they seemed to exist outside the time and space of the hotel. As night fell the sky became orange and the hotel's mirrored surface reflected it vividly. It seemed to be moving slowly in a great burning sea.

Some time in the middle of the night, Rasmussen awoke. He felt that something was wrong, a kind of nightmare amplification of the unease of an ordinary working day. The curtains had not been drawn and so the sudden presentation of the orange sky was perhaps more alarming than it might have been otherwise, but that was not what was wrong: Rasmussen rose on his elbow and looked through the dirty orange darkness to Boatman's bed. His boss was sitting bolt upright, naked, sheets tossed aside, a look of profound terror on his faintly orange face.

"Oh my god," said Boatman.

Rasmussen thought then that the building was on fire, but when he went to the window, he could see no sign of it beyond the smoky orange light. The tiny aquamarine pool below him among the crowns of darkly swaying palm trees featured a single tiny swimmer. He said that everything seemed to be okay, and looked over his shoulder at Boatman, who had fallen backward with a pop into his pillow and appeared to be asleep again—if in fact he had ever been awake. Rasmussen spoke his boss's name softly two or three times, but received no reply.

THE NEXT DAY, WITH BOATMAN ALREADY UP and gone from the room, Rasmussen rose and eased his bowels, thinking that ease was certainly not the word to characterize such a terrible struggle. He showered and shaved and dressed, slowly and carefully, giving his hangover time to subside, drank a satisfying glass of Alka-Seltzer, and settled his identification documents, color-coded stickers, and clearance badges around his neck. He rode the elevator down for some time, stopping at nearly every floor until the car was quite crowded, ambled through the thronging lobby, waved to people he knew, smiled at people he thought he knew but wasn't sure of, exited the hotel, and made his way next door to the convention center, where he rode an escalator so high into an expanse of sun-filled glass it seemed an ascent into heaven. Then he stood in a long murmuring line for a cup of coffee. Standing to one side and taking a few sips, he saw Boatman approach with another man.

Willie Masters was short and slender and impeccably dressed in a tailored three-piece suit. He looked boyish from a distance, but his face was lined and worn. His beard was full but carefully and stylishly barbered, the lenses of his glasses large and thick, aviator-like and faintly smoked, and in between two fingers an unlit cigarette twitched. Smiling broadly and engagingly, and with just enough of some kind of southern accent to make it lyrical and just enough rasp to suggest abuse of whiskey as well as tobacco, he began to speak before Boatman, who looked like a Giacometti sculpture, perhaps of Don Quixote, next to his perforce Sancho Panza-like, but dapper, lean, and cagey associate, could introduce them.

"I knew you were our man, I knew it at the bottom of the damn escalator, you practically got a halo around you, you're so damn special, I'm not kidding you, I am honestly not, you'd have to be one blind idiot of an asshole not to see how much you *do not* belong in this crowd. I'm not here to tell you how great you are even though Kyle has already told me so but I am here to tell you I can tell the damn *difference.*"

"Walter Rasmussen," said Boatman, grinning like a boy at his birthday party, "Willie Masters. Willie? Walt."

Masters shifted the cigarette to his left hand and shook Rasmussen's hand.

"Goodness *gracious,*" said Rasmussen in the voice of a southern belle in a movie, "I *do believe* I am pleased to *meet you,* Mr. Masters!"

"Oh, that's great, that's great, that's great," burbled Masters. "He's not afraid of me one little bit! I knew it! I knew it! Kyle said you were one in a million and I could see it from a quarter-mile off, you are a true human being and not one of Jack's fucking *robots.*"

"I am increasingly willing to take conversational risks," said Rasmussen, now in a musing and almost meek tone. "I don't know why."

"Oh, I can tell you why! I can most certainly and persuasively tell you why but I do not often do so because most people just do not want to know, they're afraid of it, afraid of themselves or they do not see the immediate profit in it even if they are curious, you know, and vain enough to like what they think is me kissing their ass. You're not vain, Walter, but I do know you like what you're hearing and I know you get sick to your stomach thinking about profit at all, much less immediate profit. You are too goddamn smart and it hurts to be so, is that not right. And you would rather use your heart to make decisions than your big clean-running high-horsepower Pontiac Trans-Am of a brain, is *that* not right?" They had descended the escalator and now stood on the sidewalk outside the convention center, watching buses and taxis pull up, spill and eject people from their interiors, and take off. Masters paused to light his cigarette and laugh without the slightest hint of emotional reservation or intellectual doubt in a plume of smoke. "I *know* you know I am *right.*"

"You know that I know that that is not," said Rasmussen, "*not* right."

The three men exhaled great gusts of laughter into the mild San Diego morning light. Boatman laughed the laugh of an innocent but outgoing person who has just put two interesting people together in a way that boded well for everybody's future. Masters laughed the theatrical laugh of a mad genius. Rasmussen laughed the relieved laugh of a man who was inclined to see every conversation as a precipice or a brick wall, an activity that had always called for the taking of risks. Certainly he was flattered to think he was not someone who could be flattered, and certainly he was amused; but more importantly, he was pleased to think that his boss saw him and his unsuitability to corporate life not as a liability but as, to use a phrase to which he was unsuited, an opportunity, pleased to think that friendship rather than contempt might come of their increasing familiarity with each other. It was also possible that this was the beginning of a great epoch, in which three crazy, daring men were able to break away from the bloated idiocies of a big business and act like intelligent human beings while making small fortunes doing something that was not directly inimical to the survival of the species or in aggressively bad taste. And possible, too, he had to admit it occurred to him, that they would become involved as dupes in some kind of drug trade.

Masters's rodomontade became a monologue that had no end, that could have no end because everything that happened in the immediate or greater world was tributary to it. Several hours passed between the first and second meetings of the three, but Masters spoke as if he had never ceased to speak nor Rasmussen to listen—and that was in a way nearly true. If you paid close attention, the monologue was hard on the nerves, but fascinating. Rasmussen decided he was equal to it and listened to Masters as few people in that man's life had been willing or able to listen. Boatman, perhaps strangely, seemed not to be listening, precisely, but rather to be observing Rasmussen listen. Masters was obviously an eccentric of a primary, archetypal sort, but was also obviously a polymath of stupendous proportions, psychologically keen, encyclopedically and at the same time trenchantly well informed, and emotionally sympathetic. He quoted long speeches out of Shakespeare and verses from the Bible, a vast array of postmodern thinkers, glossing them all with Enlightenment commentary, and seemed to have memorized the collected works of Ralph Waldo Emerson, about whom he could not joke.

After a while, much later that night, deeper, subtler perceptions began to accrue and take on meaning. Boatman was spellbound by Masters, and needed desperately to be involved in that way, with forces, as he thought of them, outside his experience, that would propel him beyond the slow cowboy amiability of his business savvy. Equally desperate, however, was Masters's hold on Boatman: Boatman lived in the real world as Masters did not, could not, and had done well enough that he could now speak with authority of genuine access to money and power. Boatman, Masters saw, was unformed but resourceful, good-hearted but practical, ambitious but sound. He could not penetrate the surface of the world he understood so profoundly, and Boatman's immersion in it was, in effect, just as spellbinding as his own more Barnum- and Rasputin-like charms.

Rasmussen, having reached these conclusions with drunkenly deft stumbling, and rather smugly, realized with a guilty start that a third party had confirmed what was most precious to him: his belief that he was extraordinary and not only *could be* but *should be* free of ordinary constraints. *Hold that thought,* he thought, *hold that thought,* and ordered another stiff drink, knowing that there was only one way to achieve that kind of pain-free stasis. Rather than feeling superior to Boatman and Masters, he knew he ought to be grateful, for somewhere in the convolutions of Masters's monologue and in the corner of Boatman's watchful eye was another chance to escape.

Jessie stood behind him. He looked into the mirror on the other side of the bar and there she was. She was leaning against his back and had draped her arms around his shoulders and clasped her hands over his heart. The hair piled carelessly atop her head spilled forward. She addressed him as "stud" and demanded to know how he was. He turned around on his stool while she remained excitingly where and as she was.

"I am falling in love with you."

She chuckled in a rich baritone. "Oh you are not."

She allowed herself to be hugged and kissed for a moment, then told him in no uncertain tone to stop it. She gave him a look he could not interpret, and reeled off, as if her piled-up hair had tipped her in that direction. Then suddenly she was back. She had been talking to someone from Tech Support, an urban planner like herself, who had worked for the United Nations (*yes,* she chuckled throatily, wiggling her eyebrows, *the United NATIONS*) in Tajikistan. She was *gorgeous,* a Nonya from Singapore, and might introduce him to Kofi

Annan if he pleased her in bed. She pushed away and again gave him a look that was hard to see as anything other than disgust. There was also a Polish woman who was rumored to have been a mistress of Lech Walesa. He could go fuck himself blind in Gdańsk. The name of this city she pronounced with comic stupidity, as if she were not Polish but Scandinavian, as if she were the demented Swedish fashion model she appeared to be. He would get nowhere, she went on, with Jessica Greenaway: she could display the straps of her thong all day long but would never fuck him because she was terrified of her husband. He was with County Search and Rescue, and would, you know, find them on a mountaintop. She laughed like an opera singer. Then stopped abruptly and assumed an ominous look. She whispered that Jessica's father-in-law had been a Navy SEAL and that he had given his son a .45 automatic he said he had no use for. "That was how she put it," whispered Jessie. "She said he said, 'It's just sitting around here, not doing anybody any good, Trav. You might as well take it. You never know in a search and rescue deal what might go down.'" Mystified as usual by Wunderlich's unstable conflation of hatred and desire, of intimacy and violence, but in the main untroubled, Rasmussen went up to his room.

Boatman and Masters were just settling in; they had had an interesting and encouraging day, even perhaps a provocative day in some ways, if not altogether a big day. Boatman had given up his bed for his hard-pressed friend, and Masters already had the covers drawn up to his neck. He was chain-smoking and had not ceased to talk from the moment Rasmussen had entered the room to the time he slipped into his own bed. Boatman, who had worked quite hard that day, and whose nature was simpler, fell instantly asleep, even though he was on the floor. Masters continued to talk and Rasmussen began to learn a little about who he was listening to: his maternal grandfather had been a South Carolina politician nearly the stature of Huey Long, and Masters had given many stump speeches as a child prodigy and heir apparent; he lived in a trailer in Orlando, Florida, with a hair stylist thirty years younger than himself; he had founded a business based on an astonishingly clever use of geographic information systems that Rasmussen could not quite grasp, mainly because he had so little interest in geographic information systems, but had been chiseled out of it by his mother and brother, who felt, because he had been in and out of psych wards, that he was not fit to run a business. All that was going to change, though, because Kyle Boatman was a superior human being. He was one of the innocent elect, and if he felt something surely in his heart, he would stake everything on a single throw. His (Boatman's) wife was an obstacle—not that she was not intelligent or decent, she was those things indubitably, but insofar as she was afraid of Masters. He had been sitting under a tree in their backyard, and she had observed him from the kitchen window: he had a black aura around him, he was carrying a great burden of death, and if she could not describe the nature or scope or design or direction of that death, she was convinced he was lethal. She had warned her husband, but Kyle was the real deal and would not be swayed by a hysterical and hallucinating bitch, wife or not wife. He was most certainly devoted to his wife but would not go against what he knew were überprinciples of his great soul. He would *show his wife where she was wrong and gently leach the poison from her soul.* Boatman murmured from the floor that he could not breathe with all the cigarette smoke in the room, but failed to reply when pressed for details.

Rasmussen was lulled by the gentle craziness of his roommate's biography, and found himself pleasantly adrift in alpha waves. Vaguely familiar women entered his consciousness, languidly patrolling the perimeter, occasionally drawing tantalizingly near. He confessed to Masters a desire to fuck all the women murmuring in his memory and imagination, one thousand of them over the course of one thousand nights, and when Willie Masters, whom he was quite sure would approve vigorously any notions of harem-building in the mind of the superman, surprised him by disapproving, quite somberly if not sternly, he confessed that he had not had sexual relations with anyone in a thousand nights, and that his wife had explicitly given him permission to find a young girlfriend.

"Quote unquote," he said in a stage whisper.

"She didn't mean a word of it, Walt. That was a plea for understanding and love."

"No," said Rasmussen, breaking the surface of the alpha waves with a gasp and sputtering emotionally, "no, I don't think so. I think she—"

"Don't be a fool, man!"

"I'm not! I—"

"Come on, Walt, don't bullshit a bullshitter!" He laughed rather loudly. "I don't mean *me*, brother! I mean you!" He continued to laugh. It was a pleasant and southern-accented laugh, but still remarkably loud. "Don't do it! Ha-ha-ha-ha-haaaaaa!"

"I can't breathe," mumbled Kyle Boatman. "I can't bloody breathe."

Masters lit another cigarette and took a sip from a glass of whiskey.

"She's sick to death of me," said Rasmussen softly. "Sex is the last thing she'd want with me."

"Aw, come on, Walter," Masters said gently.

A moment passed in which Rasmussen found it hard to believe he was having the kind of conversation he was having, in that place, and at that time, but then the moment was gone and he was insisting that his wife had been perfectly sincere in her observation and practical in her problem-solving. They had not been fighting, were not even in the midst of peevishness or hostility veiled as polite concern. It was simply a good idea, generously offered and humbly accepted.

"Aw, come on, man," Masters repeated. "You're talking like a complete idiot now. She was inviting you to destroy yourself."

There was a fog in the room, a stinking cloud, a miasma of delusion and perhaps depravity, or merely plain stupidity. Rasmussen looked out at the orange sky and sighed deeply. There was so little precedent for this sort of scene in his life that he didn't really know where he was. Luckily enough, he was drunk and therefore not frightened. There was a man on the floor who had hired him and could fire him, whose principal skills were in telemarketing, and a genuine lunatic coughing invisibly in a cancerous cloud in bed next to him, and yet, if there was any salience in the farce it was the ineffable, almost prelapsarian rectitude of the two clowns quietly upstaging the irremediable arrogance of the star.

BOATMAN AND MASTERS ROSE and departed early the next morning, at dawn, saying only that today was going to be the "big" day that yesterday had not quite been, the day that yesterday had steadily and thrillingly been building toward. Several hours later, as Rasmussen stood in line for the first of the ten cups of coffee he would drink that day, he saw them shoot past with a statuesque woman he didn't recognize, very attractive, very busy with communication devices. The boys were flanking her, Willie Masters laughing and talking loudly and continuously, Boatman's goateed head nodding atop his long thin body with its flapping arms and legs, the woman alternately grinning as she listened to Masters and frowning as she went back to her cell phone.

Rasmussen had a day of meetings scheduled as well. As part of his wish to be a man and do the work that had to be done, and advertise his fealty to Boatman, he had volunteered for a job no one else in the group wanted: a book demonstrating the many interesting ways that geographic information systems were being used by law enforcement agencies.

In the morning he took a short introductory course in the use of a new extension, struggled as he always did to perform even the most basic of the software's functions, realized in the course of every exercise that he was the last one to finish, that the room full of people behind him were all cops and that they were waiting for him and staring at him. The extension was something like a video game, and as the cops got familiar with the controls they began to behave like a sports team, exclaiming loudly over their victories, exhorting each other with Marine Corps-like ooo-raaahhhs, and declaring with the satisfaction of adolescents the demise of various perps and even once a bad motherfucker.

RASMUSSEN NAILED NO ONE and nothing at his monitor and felt guilty. He began to sweat and was sure he was going to be interrogated.

The first chief of police he interviewed, however, had not been in the room, and seemed even a little amusedly dismissive at the thought of the actual value of the extension. The chief was bursting with goodwill and enthusiasm that was anomalously liberal in its expression, full of ideas and plans for community outreach programs and the sharing of information. By the end of what had admittedly become a delightful conversation, Rasmussen had begun to think he might be able to put together a book describing means whereby power might be removed from law enforcement institutions as they were currently understood to exist in the most violently criminal country in the world, and entrusted to citizens. It would be all but explicitly anarchist in its general theme, and if that provoked suspicions among the sales reps who depended on government agencies for 75 percent of their sales, he would disguise it; and if it seemed far-fetched, that only fueled his desire to make it happen. And interestingly, serendipitously, it seemed to harmonize with what he had managed to grasp of the mysterious Boatman & Masters Project, which had something to do with the reversal of the flow of information from citizens into bureaucracies, with special regard to matters of real estate appraisal. He said as much to Jessie while they were having martinis and salads for lunch. She responded with sincere interest, suggesting it was cool. Then she said all Rasmussen needed now was some Red Brigade chick in a beret and sunglasses and machine gun to suck his cock.

She laughed throatily.

"How about you instead?" asked Rasmussen.

"Asshole," said Jessie. "Fuck you." And left him to pay the bill.

That night, the last of the conference, he met Willie Masters at another bar, a rowdy and noisy one in the Gaslamp Quarter of old San Diego. He spoke with unguarded enthusiasm about his book proposal, which set Masters on a nearly ungovernable course of hilarity. For the rest of the night, which was long, Masters called him "Pierre-Joseph" in honor of P.-J. Proudhon, the great French theorist who had stood up famously or infamously to Marx, calling that theorist's communism just another authoritarian religion. Masters commenced a monologue on the popular misunderstanding of Proudhon's slogan, "Property is Theft"—saying that it didn't mean any old sonofabitch could walk into your house and make a sandwich with your bread or change the channel you were watching on television or take a shit in your backyard or play his boom box in your garage—while laughing continuously and saying, "I don't have to tell *you* that, Pierre-Joseph! You're the frog motherfucker who invented it!"

A round of drinks later, Boatman appeared, making his way excitedly through the crowd with the tall good-looking woman, who was letting him lead her by the elbow while she spoke on her cell phone. Boatman and Masters conferred inaudibly in the din, and when the woman concluded her conversation and slipped her phone into her purse, the two men stood and all three engaged in elaborate and comic slappings of the palm and heartfelt embraces. She passed something to Boatman, smiled at Rasmussen, and departed.

Boatman let out a whoop that attracted notice and laughter from nearby tables, where most of the people were fellow employees and especially close customers, and he informed a sardonic waitress that he was buying a round for everybody, indicating the tables he meant with a lordly sweeping gesture. Rasmussen demanded jovially to know what had happened, and a good deal of drunken talk ensued. As the night wore on, however, it became clear that nothing had happened. Or, rather, that the woman had slipped Boatman a hundred-dollar bill to subsidize the evening's consumption of alcohol.

"Free bee-ah," said Kyle Boatman. He winked, but was quite serious in his insider's estimation of the actual value and deeper ramifications—entirely positive, he insisted, sensing some vague negativity in the depths of the word—of the many branchings of consequence from the solid, healthy, massive trunk of free beer.

[5]

TRAGEDY STRUCK THE GROUP, obliquely, but immediately after the close of the conference. It was the first death they would confront, but not the last. Jess Papantonio had gone to San Francisco with her husband, an architect who was interviewing for a job that they believed he would be offered and that would allow them to flee Southern California. Jess's younger brother already lived in San Francisco, and they were staying with him. A gifted and accomplished young man with startling access to the aristocracy of the Bay Area, he was an amateur triathlete as well. The morning after Jess arrived, he went out for an eight-mile run, up and down the famously steep hills of the city. When he returned, he stood on the sidewalk outside his house and gave directions to North Beach to his sister, then collapsed and died. Rasmussen heard the news that afternoon, taking a call from Jess in his office, where he was hunting leads for his law enforcement project. He had never met the brother, but in not much more than a year, Jess had become the kind of friend that made it impossible for him to not feel a good deal of the force of the blow as well. He walked into her office and looked at the picture of Jess and her brother. Their faces were large and distorted; they had likely been holding the camera themselves, but the effect, of course, was to magnify their toothy smiles.

Boatman and Masters were working that Saturday, too; they were preparing themselves for a meeting with the founder, and had been doing so ceaselessly since their triumphant return from the conference. To what specific end they toiled, however, remained a mystery, at least to Rasmussen, who thought the pair were acting like boys in a tree-fort clubhouse. It was likely, given Boatman's wife's antipathy, that Willie was sleeping in Boatman's office, sneaking showers at Boatman's when the coast was clear, and his sharp-looking suit had begun to look like a sack, but he was as cheerfully voluble as ever and a welcome alternative to Boatman, who was increasingly haggard and nervous, as he played, Rasmussen suspected, even further from the rules than his usual standards of business acumen allowed.

Having wandered numbly into the wing's common area and kitchen, Rasmussen saw Boatman exit the men's room and take a long, exhausted-seeming drink at the fountain, braced over it and pausing between drinks to sigh deeply. He finished, turned, and angled across the space but apparently did not notice Rasmussen, then opened a door and went down the hallway to his office.

Rasmussen thought reflexively that Kyle Boatman was a friend, and if a little voice warned that he was not exactly a friend, he was Jess's boss and a decent human being with whom the terrible news ought to be immediately shared. And Willie Masters, though he was not acquainted with Jess, much less with her brother, would naturally be stricken, sympathetically, to think someone so young had died, of such a cause. He went to Boatman's office.

"Jess's brother died," he said.

Both men looked at him distractedly, impatiently. "Who?" asked Boatman.

"Jess."

"Jess?"

116

"Yes. Her brother."

"Which Jess . . .? Her brother . . .?"

Rasmussen saw that Boatman did not care who had died. It was possible he had revealed an actual dislike for Jess Papantonio as well. Rasmussen's knees became weak and wobbly, his hands began to tremble, and his face to burn.

"Jess Papantonio," he said. "Her brother. He was training for a triathlon and collapsed after a run and died."

Masters said nothing but continued to look at Rasmussen. Boatman cleared his throat after a moment and stood up. He gently moved Rasmussen away from his office, toward the kitchen. "Look," he said, "I can't really think about that right now. Okay? I mean, tell Jess I'm sorry and everything, but . . . okay?"

Rasmussen nodded. Boatman clapped him on the shoulder and left. Jess never returned to her office, not even to collect her photographs.

SOME MONTHS PASSED. As little appeared to come of the Boatman & Masters Project as of Rasmussen's *Anarchism and Geographic Information Systems*. Like the book on sustainable development and remote sensing, his revolutionary fantasies degenerated swiftly into marketing patter. Digital maps describing crime hot spots in real time seemed to be the extent of current usage: as police department budgets dwindled and violent crime overtook the nation, GIS software could help law enforcement officials bring their limited resources to bear where they were most needed and would be most effective. Midyear reviews came and went without so much as a blink from Boatman in the direction of Rasmussen's recent efforts—a blink being understood as perforce admonitory, its absence a kindness given the laziness and failure that even the most cursory scrutiny would reveal. Looking back at his earlier work, Rasmussen hoped he could return to the college, high school, and grade school texts with which he had debuted so brilliantly, and was deeply chagrined to be told that Livia Barker was now their "K-12 education specialist." Perhaps as a result of this perhaps minor but nevertheless embittering blow, but also perhaps as well the cause of it, Rasmussen's self-confidence and sense of physical well-being—imperiled most obviously by a tremendous gain of weight—guttered dangerously. He found himself angrily grieving most of the day, and could snap out of it only by going out for drinks with a select group of like-minded co-workers: for instance the demigoddess Satyavati; her desperately ill husband, Winston, who despite the constant shadow of death had the wish and the will to be, the satiric resources, the timing, and the command of the room of a stand-up comic; Sati's adoring sidekick, Amber Winklemann, the plump and pretty former star student of Rasmussen's wife, for whose employment as a proofreader Rasmussen had lobbied strenuously when she failed the copyediting test, arguing simply but effectively that she was one of the most intelligent and hardworking young persons he had ever met; Edward Cage, whose intolerance of alcohol was matched only by his game efforts to stay at the table; and the two supermodels, Jessie and Jessica, who vied cattily for supremacy. During the course of these evenings of drink, he would feel again and again that he had rediscovered the meaning of life. It was ridiculously simple. One was to find ways to shout with laughter and not care so much about world affairs and one's role in those affairs. It was nearly unbelievable how jolly one could become if one adopted such a philosophy. His wife failed to see it that way, and left to spend the summer with her brother's family in Boston, a separation, she suggested, that would be a good way to initiate a legally binding one. And so it was, in that spirit of heedless revelry and the satiation of animal appetites turning inexorably with the dawn into weakness and despair only to return, grimly, weakly, with the setting sun, to the reckless indulgence of various lusts, hysterias, and that most dangerous of all untruths, the truth ever so slightly distorted, that Rasmussen took up with Jessica Greenaway, exactly twenty years his junior, with whom he had spent many productive and enjoyable working hours, and commenced the destruction of his life.

[6]

AS RASMUSSEN DESCENDED, so rose the cartographer Anita Portolan. If everyone on the team was more or less important, Anita was more important. While the others were certainly geniuses in their own ways, there was typically only one thing they could do, and Anita could do everything. Extremely witty (rarely to the point of cruelty) and sensitive (rarely to the point of vengeance) she was a scientist and an artist both, well versed in human nature and methods of organization on the enterprise, departmental, small group, and individual levels. She had been a coxswain on an unbeaten crew at McGill in Montreal and had Kyle Boatman wrapped around her little finger in a matter of weeks. Boatman seemed quite clearly to enjoy this, and Anita was adroit enough to make sure that he felt he was still the boss, no matter how effective she might be seen to be here and there around the company. A faint stink of sadomasochistic eroticism worked its way into the cracks and seams of things. Rasmussen had not only sailed irreconcilably past the headlands of his wife's understanding by then, he had lost his bearings completely in a stormy sea of alcoholic hilarity and violence, and so, consequently, did not notice when the complicated relationship between Anita and Boatman took on a life of its own and lapsed from their control. Nor did he understand the nature of the malignancy it actually manifested.

One of the great perquisites of the year was the annual Convention of American Booksellers. The splendor of this meeting has since deliquesced, but in those days, just as independent

GARY AMDAHL

publishers were being purchased by conglomerates, there was a great deal of money spent in the service of publicity: breakfasts with famous authors, free brunches and lunches, dinners and after-dinner speakers, readings, signings, panel discussions, and more free books than any single person could haul. To these events Boatman doled out tickets secretly, to persons in favor. His thinking in the matter was hard to penetrate; evidently there weren't enough tickets to go around, but it seemed mainly the women who were excluded, along with Cage, whose principled stances were beginning to bore Boatman and some of the more businesslike members of the team, and Rasmussen, who was, not surprisingly, considered increasingly unstable and best left to his own devices and resources. Strangely, even Anita was denied these freebies. Strangely because she was clearly second in command, but even more strangely because a book she was co-author of was up for a prize, to be awarded at one of the more prestigious dinners, and was being energetically promoted at the company's booth. When she asked if there might not be some kind of general pass she might use, Boatman with rueful commiseration said no, there was no such thing, even though exactly such a thing existed in his briefcase, an identification tag and pass with Anita's name on it, shortly to be slung around the neck of someone posing as "Anita Portolan, Guest Author": Boatman's wife, who would be forced, in the course of the day, to accept congratulations for her fine book.

The thinking here was even more difficult to sketch out, since nearly everyone agreed that very little thinking had actually occurred. One hypothesis advanced as an essential presupposition the idea that some sort of subconscious and neurotic confusion of the two women was at work in Boatman's brain. Around this centrality almost anything could swarm: the guilt of a man obsessed with monogamy who had fallen for a smooth operator, a perverse desire to have his wife in effect "dress up," a genuinely actionable instance of sexual harassment in the workplace, or—this one had the best

120

odds—a simplemindedly fraudulent exercise of power, a scheme hatched in the middle of a sleepless night by a man fearing for his captaincy.

When the treachery was discovered—a slip of the tongue by a garrulous aide-de-camp—Anita reserved a conference room, escorted Boatman to it, invited him (tersely, it is true) to take a seat, then worked him over like a prosecuting attorney. Denying her more than three times (isn't it *true,* isn't it *true,* isn't it *true?*), Boatman finally sobbed a confession and begged for leniency on the grounds that his job was too difficult for one man to handle.

"Apologize to the team and I won't go to Human Resources."

"Done."

The apology was candid in its tone but false, or at least misleading and obfuscatory, in its depiction of misdemeanors committed against the team by its leader. It only confused the team, but confusion and the deflection of a solid blow to his midsection had been Boatman's primary intent. He followed it with a blow of his own: he went to Human Resources himself, on the principle that whoever calls the cops first, wins. He would have to confess to the misuse of company resources, but he would nail Anita for coercion. They would both get a spanking but hers would hurt more because it would take her by surprise and she would fall from a great height of moral superiority with only righteousness to cushion her.

It was a superb move; as Boatman laid low and unofficial news of it made its way through the team (company policy forbade discussion and even the appearance of knowledge of the action), there was a week of unrest, and, in some quarters, incredulity and indignation capped by a round of speeches expressing outrage and pity, but the clearest consequence was the gradual but remorseless shunning, and eventual expulsion from the team, of Anita Portolan. Though no one said so, perhaps could not have said, the knowledge being instinctive, it was understood that an attempt on the life of a superior was, if you could not guarantee the outcome—a killing—a lethally foolish undertaking. It mattered not at all that Anita had been trying to do the right thing. It mattered not at all that Anita had not wished to wound, much less depose, Boatman, but only to insist that he acknowledge his own gross stupidity and apologize for it. It mattered not at all that this was a neighbor talking to a neighbor, a friend to a friend, rather than calling the cops. It mattered not at all that Anita was virtuous and Boatman vicious. Though she and Satyavati Swenson and Amber Winklemann appeared to remain close, nearly inseparable friends, and stepped up, if anything, the amplitude of complaint at the daily bitchfests on the balcony, Sati had begun a careful realignment of her position in the company, as well as a kind of rearmament of herself that struck Rasmussen as not at all Buddhist in theory or practice, but quite effective politically. She was nobody's fool, but it gave him pause. Amber Winklemann developed an imitation of Anita that was basically a set of variations on the theme of regal condescension; Rasmussen would sometimes glance up and see her in midpose in someone's office, the other occupants convulsed in the wickedness of it.

Then a rumor began to circulate that Cage, exercising his ethical will over Anita with preternatural force, had precipitated the whole affair. This rumor, once established, fostered a lurking belief that Cage was suicidally in love with Anita, that once his mesmeric hold on her began to fail, he would use a gun to blow his brains out all over her office. Those few who knew of his many violently unhappy marriages, his years of therapy, and the hard-won but true peace that now reigned in his soul—Rasmussen and Anita, most notably—dismissed these observations and prophecies with scorn, but were secretly troubled when he bought her a DVD player (a gift accepted by Anita's heavily muscled boyfriend with good-humored nonchalance) and other expensive gifts—and seemed unable or unwilling to hear other people speaking to him when she was near.

Rasmussen, meanwhile, had nearly removed himself from the solar system, so remote was his sensing. He was in an orbit beyond Pluto, so deep that he appeared stationary, a tiny, fixed star in a constellation whose mythic references centered on the image of a man laughing himself to death. His wife returned from Boston, put divorce on the table, asked him to find and make an appointment with a marriage counselor just for the hell of it, and to move out, with the understanding that he would get custody of their two dogs when the separation became permanent. A billion miles away, he was nevertheless stung with guilt and remorse—that is the nature of the universe—and quickly got them in to see someone, who introduced them to the Buddhist idea of mindfulness, urging them to see themselves as crystalline containers of pure clear water and a layer of sediment that left undisturbed would rest on the bottoms of the containers but that would, disturbed by anger, make the water filthy and impenetrable. This turned out to have a great deal of meaning for Rasmussen, who'd had no idea how turbid he was, even with Sati's preparatory dharma talks, but very little for his wife. She described his new friends as having "no idea what they're getting into," and apparently devoted to him only because they had "no idea who he actually was." At one point he peered at her through the murk and sludge with what he thought was flabbergasted frustration only to have her shout, *"I'm not afraid of you anymore!"*

The idea that she'd ever once been afraid of him was preposterous and he laughed a laugh of (he thought) baffled outrage. A nice, cheap apartment nearby came up for rent and he jumped, even though he'd not be allowed to bring his dogs there. He was devoted to his dogs, but somehow the actual gravity of the situation escaped him, and he accustomed himself to life in a bachelor's pad (this was a phrase from his childhood that would forever stand for the place where a man could be free) as if he were a character not in a Russian novel but in a television comedy. He ate cheap, ridiculously packaged food that had almost no protein or fiber in it, signed up for satellite dish reception so he could watch forty hockey games a week (it reminded him of home), and almost never moved from one of the most comfortable couches he'd ever lain upon. Whenever the evening was free for such activity, he drank himself into befuddlement, and made contingency plans to seduce a hundred women in the coming year, if the tireless but still mystifying Jessica should for some reason fall by the wayside. That there would soon come a time when he was afraid to leave the couch did not seem possible, and the thought of becoming permanently befuddled did not trouble him in the least, as he saw quite clearly that when he was befuddled, he didn't care, and that when he was not befuddled, he looked forward to it, preferred it to the witty vigilance of his former character. Jessica facilitated the affair by separating from her searching and rescuing husband of not quite one year, getting him, as Rasmussen's wife had gotten Rasmussen, to move out, and securing what was in effect a restraining order, emphatic and severe but not administered or guaranteed by the police. She also suggested that they run away to Seville, in the country of Spain.

Strange things began to happen to him. Arising from an afternoon nap, he walked into the bathroom to urinate, got perhaps halfway through the business, and fainted. During a lunch break at a conference, he strolled to a park, lay down in the grass, and slept for four hours, awaking in the dusk among other bums. Erectile dysfunction was upon him like a curse. A sleepless night of mounting anxiety left him unable to do anything but gasp with relief when his flight was canceled—and rather than rush to get another flight, he simply went home. The next time he was to go to the airport, the flight was not canceled but he found himself unable to board it, as he had fainted again in his bathroom. Under ordinary circumstances, such failures would have caused concern and inquiry and decisions about what had been at stake, what had been lost, what irretrievably, and what not. These were not, however, ordinary circumstances. The seminar that Rasmussen had missed was not of particular importance, but the man who was offering it was of great importance: he had invented geographic information systems. To be fair to Rasmussen, he'd thought he was blowing off anonymous attendance at a seminar, not a meeting with the great man . . . but the great man, it turned out, had been waiting for him. Boatman's team was assembling a kind of Festschrift in his honor, publishing a memoir of his career, and collecting his aphorisms, and this was a step in the wrong direction. Boatman said it sent the wrong signal when he and Rasmussen talked it over. He was very sympathetic and reassuring, however, concluding that no real damage had been done (the inventor had called the founder and the founder had called Boatman), but did suggest that Rasmussen might actually welcome removal from this particular project.

"Yes," agreed Rasmussen, "I would indeed. All we really need to do is hook a tape recorder up to the old man's asshole, and have somebody in Office Resources transcribe it."

"Right," grinned Boatman. And still grinning, he said, "You know, when you called in sick, and said you were embarrassed, I think that was the word, or ashamed, that you'd, you know, *passed out*, and didn't want me to tell anybody, well, I didn't tell anybody."

"You didn't tell anybody." It wasn't quite sinking in, what that meant.

"No. But if we just slip you off the project, no damage will have been done."

"I see."

"And you do not in fact want the project, right?"

It was sinking in, but Rasmussen shook his head. No damage would be done.

In fact a great deal of damage had been done, by both men, but both men, in very different ways, remained oblivious of or unconcerned by the damage of his own making, focusing instead,

125

GARY AMDAHL

secretly, on the damage the other was responsible for. Thus concluded the second act of the tragedy.

[7]

THE AFFAIR, SWIFTLY GIVEN OVER to sudden and unpredictable descents into the most primitive emotional states that were like wildfires, flash floods, riptides, and tornadoes in their remorselessness and power to devastate, and the clear but never admitted understanding that this was a great example of the kind of relationship the French have an untranslatable word for (it suggests the sudden appearance of a bridge over which one has crossed but not known was there) was balanced by indescribable pleasures and a sense of dangerous adventure that was, curiously, like watching a deftly manipulative but not especially good movie.

One night, a very hot night in the middle of the summer (the temperature would still be above ninety at midnight), Jessica was working late and her husband called her. The agreement was that he would call her when he wanted to see her, and she would either accept the visit or decline it.

"Where are you?" he asked.

"I'm at work."

"No you're not."

"I beg your pardon?"

"You're not at work. Where are you? I want to see you."

"*I am at work.*"

"*No you are not. I am standing in the courtyard of your building, next to the koi pond, and I can see your office and the light is NOT ON. WHERE THE FUCK ARE YOU?*"

Jessica often worked with low light or no light, finding that light interfered with accurate perception of color on her monitor

126

screen. She set the phone down, flicked the light on, and went to her window. She couldn't see her estranged husband, but made a dismissive gesture with both hands, remaining in that pose for quite some time. When she got back to her phone, her husband had hung up. She imagined him reeling through the night, choking back sobs, and began to cry herself.

Rasmussen had been working late, too, but had gone over to the company's little gym, determined to fully re-create in himself the twenty-five-year-old he had once so promisingly been. He had been flat-stomached, ripplingly muscled, and an accomplished (produced) playwright. He had actually spent his twenty-fifth year living on the money he'd made from a production of *Fall Down Go Boom* and a state arts grant. There was a photograph from that time that he kept in a drawer in his office, him on stage offering some dramaturgical cogency or emotional blandishment to a beautiful young actress dressed only in ballet tights. Rasmussen wore a wife-beater T-shirt, ripped jeans, a frayed straw cowboy hat and pointy boots. He was smoking a cigar and his forearms were right out of a comic book. The photo sometimes amused him, sometimes caused him to feel some fondness for himself, but most often caused angry tears to well in his eyes: that he could have thought so smugly well of himself made him want to bang his head against a wall; and that vestiges of that esteem should still exist troubled him deeply. But was there not something else going on there? Was there not something actually quite good, quite valuable, quite laudable? They were supposed to be ridiculously vain. They were supposed to make foolish spectacles of themselves. They were supposed to indulge in whatever caprice or desire happened to cross their paths—*and in the service of what were they supposed to do these things?* Sure, you could say "entertainment" and get punitively biblical about it—or you could say they were acting in the service of understanding. Yes: you could be as dopey and tragic and frivolous and tormented as you wanted, so long as you could retain a kind of dignity in the spotlight and make sure the audience understood what you were talking about. Pluck your eyes out in horror at what you've done, complain about your family, tie a widow to the railroad tracks, escape from a dungeon—*anything at all,* so long as you were clear about it. Yes. Yes indeed. All those histrionics, all those tantrums and poses and humiliations—they banded together and went through all that for a few spotlit moments of clarity.

Rasmussen looked at the picture and admitted he was a fool. He agreed he was probably not a good man in the usual ways. But he did believe he had tried to be otherwise. He believed it so ardently that when Jessica, weeping, found him in the gym, his face was streaked as well. They talked for a few minutes and he comforted her to a small but acceptable degree, only to have his work undone by the sound of someone banging on the door.

It was of course Jessica's husband, Travis, and he demanded they come outside.

"I saw you smelling my wife's hair," he said. The gym was in a little building of its own, and mostly walled with glass. In the dark hot night it glowed like a cold jewel, or a television set. Travis was dripping sweat. His chest was heaving and his eyes were burning red.

"You *what?*" asked Rasmussen.

"I used to *like* you, man!" shouted Travis. "But not anymore!"

It was a perfectly confounding thing to say, and all Rasmussen could do was stare at the young man. Then he rolled his eyes and threw his arms up in despair.

"Look," he said, "I'm going to give you some advice and you can listen to me or not. But you had better start listening to your wife because you are going to lose her, you have lost her, and you're going to lose her for good and all you'll be able to think about is what an asshole you are and how badly you want her back, but it won't happen and the only reason it won't happen is because you refused to fucking listen to her."

They all fell silent for a moment. An owl screeched overhead, and palm fronds crackled faintly in a hot puff of wind.

"Come on," said Travis. "Let's go home."

"*No,*" said Jessica. "I'm not going anywhere with you."

Travis stepped back and again all were silent.

"FUCKING BITCH!" he bellowed. "I JUST THOUGHT WE COULD PLAY SOME AIR HOCKEY TOGETHER!" He spun away, literally spinning, staggering, and jogged across the parking lot, appearing and disappearing as he made his way from pool of light to pool of light. Rasmussen thought with helpless sadness, he is just a more stupid version of my twenty-five-year-old self. We even look alike. And because he knew this characterization of another person, a fellow sufferer, as "stupid" was less an effect of his arrogance than it was of his own greater, or at least grosser, stupidity, he felt suddenly bankrupt and more than a little desperate for some kind of psychological re-funding. Then an old proverb drifted into his thoughts, Spanish or Portuguese, possibly Sicilian or Neapolitan, Alfonso the Magnanimous? *Trust in the power of the deed once you have carried it out.* Something like that. It was either that or whimpering and whining. Smell the twerp's wife's hair. Fuck the wife. Fuck other men's wives and girlfriends and mothers and daughters, fuck them all until you got tired of fucking, it happens but it doesn't last long, and you can eat and sleep in the meantime. When raiders from other villages sneak up, or outraged twerps from your own, scare them back the way they came. If they pretend to boldness, kill them. Yes, killing was for better or worse part of being an alpha male and he had better get used to the idea. *All men are courageous. Only one man is courageous at the last moment.*

EPISODES LIKE THAT (there were several) alternated with orgasms in unexpected places, drunken and gratuitous denunciations of character—either maudlin or vicious, or, rarely but superbly, both—and clownishly just situations in which Rasmussen, and not Travis, was staked through the heart with jealousy: endless parades of cool young men from the cool and well-paid technological brains of the company, in and out of Jessica's office. Jessie Wunderlich would tremble with rage at the carefree success of Jessica's no more than comparable good looks but more wickedly wholesome seductiveness, but Jessica would grin and make a cheerful joke, then kick back in her chair and spread her legs as if to say *it is a dreamily spectacular cunt, just as you suspect, it can grant you three wishes and I'll give you a minute to think about what you really want, but then you'll have to get out because you are drooling on my page proofs.* And Rasmussen would find pretexts to enter the scene and assert his supremacy, which invariably failed, met as they invariably were by Jessica's reflexive wish to stifle any rumors that they were seeing each other by exclaiming every time he drew near, "Oh no. What do *you* want." Which fooled everyone: Rasmussen was just another uncle, some aged asshole who edited shit for the loss-leading dream team of the too-clever and weirdly zealous Aussie, Boatman. *What do YOU want?* and everybody would laugh the office laugh, but the young men, they couldn't hide it, they would dart glances at Rasmussen; and after a while he began getting anonymous phone calls from young men with distorted voices asking him was she as good as she looked. Rasmussen complained about being an alpha male who had to pretend he was a twerp, but Jessica would have none of it. *Those boys get to line up and describe their exploits and write me disguised love poems, Richard Gelb gets a nickname, Kyle Boatman gets to take all kinds of liberties while he pries into my personal life and advises me on the deep greatness of marriage, and you get to sleep with me.*

It was during this tense and dramatic time as well that Travis's best friend and fellow searcher-and-rescuer moved into the house next door to Rasmussen's. It was the kind of ridiculously far-fetched coincidence that you had to expect, after all, in what was in effect a small town, but find hard to believe in a work of fiction. Because Rasmussen had moved out, he almost never saw Travis, who, having of course moved out too, was staying with his grandmother and so spent a lot of time drinking with his friend. Occasionally, when Rasmussen came to walk his dogs, they would glare at each other from driveway to driveway, but never speak. Jessica was adamant in her description of Rasmussen as a close friend with whom she could talk, freely and safely, which left Travis with only the certain knowledge of betrayal, its cold dark shape, but no evidence over which he might justifiably go apeshit. The glare from a medium distance was his only weapon. Once he parked his car so close to Rasmussen's in the grocery store lot that Rasmussen had to get in on the passenger's side, and once, standing atop a ladder propped against the side of his friend's garage, where he was rigging up a motion detector for the yard light, he was able to spit across the tiny lawn to within forty or fifty feet of the dog-walking Rasmussen, who absorbed these beta antics with the calm and confident strength of one who has completely lost sight of moral land but who believes himself to be, and informs in a grandiose but moving speech the crew, his little audience of selves, that they are en route to the Indies and stupendous wealth. He laughed. But he was worried Travis might say something threatening to his wife; if that happened, things—even though he saw it clearly in the distance he was powerless to turn away—would quickly and uncontrollably deteriorate.

The end of the affair came about with both a whimper and a bang. Jessica was a great proponent of amusement, of relaxed and lighthearted pleasure. She read books but was overly secretive about it, and though it turned out she had firm, broadly conservative political opinions, she preferred the jocular and the droll to any sort of more substantive discussion. She enjoyed television comedy and movies that were blatantly ridiculous, or, as she saw it, unpretentious. Rasmussen tried to get her to watch his favorite movie, *Slap Shot*, but she was less and less enthusiastic as the movie wore on, sensing a seriousness underneath the admittedly goofy, raunchy surface that unsettled and ultimately displeased her. Rasmussen was glad he had not suggested his second favorite, *Andrei Rublev*. She liked very much, perhaps more than anything else in the world, to sunbathe poolside and sip cool sweet rum drinks. Las Vegas was her favorite city, Los Angeles her least. She liked to surf, and had done quite a lot of it while attending college in San Diego, but liked more the use of personal watercraft on the Colorado River—even though, or perhaps because, Rasmussen had come eventually to suspect— her first love had died in just that way. She was, in other words, in these outward aspects, exactly the sort of person Rasmussen was in the habit of despising. But just as the old joke had it, he "became the sort of person he hated and was much happier." The true quality of that happiness, its nature and depth, remained in question, but the facsimile was good for at least a couple of months, at the end of which the odd couple went to a concert given by the laid-back pop sensation Jimmy Buffett. This was a crucial intersection of character and history: many years earlier, when Rasmussen was in his early twenties and Jessica an infant, one of his best friends had returned from four years as a gunner's mate in the U.S. Navy, with three or four long-playing record albums of Nashville country music as transformed by Key West, by a Mississippian who seemed to personify an American spiritual ideal: the gentle, lazy, sweet, continuous abuse of any controlled substances and anal legalities near to hand. The guitarist and balladeer lived in a hammock, rode a bicycle around his island town, and performed for drinks in local bars. Money meant nothing to him, he had said so, clearly and beautifully, in one of his most famous and endearing songs. He was intelligent, like older country and western swingers had been, Hank Williams, for example, or at least not defiantly stupid, as country stars had become, Hank Williams Jr., for example; he had novelists for friends, novelists on Rasmussen's private list of serious literary artists! There were too many splendid confluences for him and his friends to resist

Buffett, and so he was a staple of their youth; but that Buffett should still be alive, still be a force for good in the world, and an object of fervent adoration for Jessica Greenaway—that seemed a gift from gods who were all in favor of Rasmussen becoming twenty-five years old again, and who were determined, in their mighty, if ominously inscrutable, ways, to make it happen.

Things, of course, had changed in America, but because those changes had been concurrent with Rasmussen's disappearance into middle age, he had not noticed them.

Because Travis was only partially successful in concealing his stalking of the woman he still loved more than life itself, because he was sincere where he needed to be subtle, but was as grimly determined as the undercover narcotics detective or border patrolman he hoped one day he might somehow become, a great deal of subterfuge was engaged in as absolutely necessary preparation for the concert. A decoy trip to Las Vegas was planned and old friends of the couple were instructed in elaborate lies that would not satisfy but might possibly stall Travis when he reasoned that no force on earth could keep Jessica from a Jimmy Buffett concert: *she was a parrothead.*

Rasmussen did not know what a "parrothead" was; nor had he realized that "Margaritaville," once merely a clever reference to alcoholic indolence, was now a corporate entity. That someone in the entertainment industry who romanticized carefree poverty should have become one of the richest men in America was just one of many things that should not have surprised Rasmussen (that was in fact the title of a memoir he'd been writing for many years: *I Don't Know Why I'm Surprised*), but he was surprised, bitterly surprised. He felt foolish, embarrassed, and drank sweet rum drinks (Buffett's own brand) as fast as he could to disguise his discomfiture, his growing shame that it, his life, had come to this, and he had allowed himself to be present at such a gathering. Luckily, everyone seemed to feel the same way—ashamed at the lengths to which they had gone to be amused—and had adopted the same method of coping—fraternity house levels of intoxication—but this kind of mass self-deceit seemed only to be undoing their ability to remain amused: there was a dangerous current of hostility running through every exchange of favorite song lyrics or bottle of Buffett Beer. In this way it was no different than a stock-car race or football game or election or war: one was there to support the team; and the team in turn assuaged the superficial loneliness and underlying, almost infrastructural fear of metastasizing anomie that was the cross every white wealthy Christian had to bear, and that sometimes was used in place of a spine. Everywhere that people were encouraged to support a team, overconsumption of alcohol was frankly encouraged as well, along with the primitive but inarguably effective means of frightening enemies, the painting of one's face. The bonus here was that men could wear coconut bras and grass skirts and women nothing but leis and bikini bottoms.

The concert was being held outdoors, in northern San Diego County. This was like going from the frying pan, for one of the liberal elite like Rasmussen, into the fire. This was one of the strongholds of the Angry White Men of 1994, the increasingly obese little boys who had turned their molten wrath at not being able to ride their tricycles in wilderness areas into stunning, literally stunning, political power. That much was clear to anyone studying demographics; but anecdotally, Rasmussen had deeper knowledge: he knew, with the clarity that comes of fight-or-flight adrenaline saturation, that he could pick any Weekend Warrior motor home/luxury recreation vehicle of the thousand strung together with hammocks and leis, walk into it, and see a poorly reproduced photograph of Martin Luther King Jr., with the slogan SHOOT SIX MORE AND GET THE WHOLE WEEK OFF.

The sun set and hours of bleary hysteria passed. Vegas production values were somewhat lost in the rolling hills, but the music and between-numbers patter was broadcast well enough that Rasmussen could hear it over the screaming of the people around him, most noticeably Jessica, who seemed to be struggling with demons out of a painting by Hiëronymus Bosch, bent on suppressing her love for Jimmy. She shrieked and wailed like the girls who were the first to encounter the Beatles at Shea, like men who have won ATVs on game shows, like any person in the United States in the grip of fun.

DRIVING HOME, THE COOLER and more ironically sophisticated Jessica resumed control.

"I see," she said. "Woodstock Nation was a good thing, Raider Nation is a bad thing. Have I got that right?"

"Woodstock was about peace and love and understanding," Rasmussen blurted helplessly, and Jessica snorted. "Raider Nation is about hate and fear and—"

"And *football.*"

"It's not about football."

"It's about hate and fear," minced Jessica.

"Yes," insisted Rasmussen. "Xenophobic family values."

"Okay, so you're going to what, hold a candlelight vigil until football has been outlawed?"

"*Why Are We in Vietnam?*"

"What?"

"Never mind."

"We're not in Vietnam!"

"Never mind. It's a novel—"

"Anybody who *was* in Vietnam, defending your right to hold candlelight vigils against the evils of football, *got spat on.*"

"No they didn't."

"*Oh yes they did.*"

"That's a myth. Propagated by—"

"Tell that to my father."

135

"Your father was in Vietnam?"

"*Oh he certainly was.*"

"They stopped the draft a year before I became eligible."

"Yes?"

"I was ready to go to Canada."

Jessica said nothing for quite a long time. They passed through the Immigration and Naturalization Service checkpoint, cleverly concealed forty miles into American territory, on I-15, between Escondido and Temecula, were instantly recognized in the blindingly intense light as flag-and-Bible folk, and waved through. The light was actually so strong going through the lenses of windshields that the features of the faces of occupants of other cars were distorted, blurred or softened or erased altogether, as if their faces had been painted, in support of the team, with thick white paint. They drove into the darkness and Jessica said, sniffling and wiping away a tear, that she didn't know why she was surprised.

"I'm just glad," sang Rasmussen in a Mississippi accent he had perfected while watching *Eyes on the Prize*, "that you all let Negroes play in the white leagues now. They're tremendously gifted athletes. The standard of play has risen dramatically. When I was a boy—"

"Oh why don't you just shut the fuck up about when you were a boy, will you please?"

"*—segregation was the law of the land. The game is much the better fah integration.*"

"You make speeches all day long about the *value of community* and how it takes a village but when you actually encounter a community, you piss on it."

Because he had a gift for sarcasm and humorous voices, Rasmussen thought he might go on for a bit, but something inside him reached its capacity, and remorse began to flow through him, followed by sorrow that was like a tide he could not resist, and then suddenly, the realization that he had had enough of himself, too.

PEASANTS

AFTER THE GROTESQUERIE AND THUDDING tumult of the concert, and the droning lacerations and silent grief of the drive home, Jessica's house was cool and quiet, and they entered it as they would a refuge. They talked quietly, something like the friends they had been and might yet be again, until they were tired. Jessica asked Rasmussen to stay, and they fell quickly, deeply, relievedly, gratefully asleep.

RASMUSSEN DREAMED OF A GREAT DRUM being slowly but steadily beaten, in a solemn, dirgelike rhythm. Then it began to quicken and he became uneasy. Then the light was on and Travis was standing in the doorway. He looked like a ghost but Rasmussen was unafraid.

"Oh, Travis," he sighed disappointedly.

Then Jessica, naked, was shouting at him, and Travis's ghost disappeared. The house shook when he slammed the front door. Jessica and Rasmussen threw on clothes and went into the living room. Jessica opened the front door.

"He ran that way," she said, looking back over her shoulder at Rasmussen.

"For Pete's sake," said Rasmussen, inclined to softpedal in times of serious threat and emergencies.

She stepped out on the porch. "Oh no, he's kicking your car."

They could hear Travis howling with rage halfway down the quiet street, and the thumps of his assault on Rasmussen's car.

"He can kick my car around all night if he wants."

"Should I call the police?"

"No."

"Here he comes."

Jessica stepped outside to intercept him, and all Rasmussen could make out for a few moments was that Travis wanted to talk. Then Jessica was screaming that he was hurting her, and Rasmussen slammed the screen door open, ripping it from its hinges and knocking Travis off the porch into the bushes. Then suddenly the three of them were in the living room and Jessica was on the phone. She was dripping blood all over it, and her face was covered with blood. Travis and Rasmussen were locked in a nearly silent, nearly immobile struggle, grunting and heaving. Rasmussen had said more than once that he was not going to fight. Travis had swung his fists ineffectually about himself a few times, clipping Rasmussen's ear and landing two or three darkly comic *thunks* to the top of his head, but now they were almost perfectly still. The longer it went on, the more ragged but the more slow their breathing became. Rasmussen again insisted he was not going to fight, but was bending Travis's finger backward and was about to break it when Travis sprang away from him. Rasmussen felt, but could not identify, the feeling that would nevertheless from that moment never leave him, that he did not want to hurt Travis because Travis was his son. But he followed in Travis's wake, pushing him into an antique hutch, which cracked and splintered, of plates and knickknacks, which broke into hundreds of pieces, and then, spinning away from the mess, smashing his face into a framed picture, which shattered, the shards opening wounds in several places on Travis's face. They stood panting for a moment, dripping blood and sweat, and then Travis left.

The police came, and the paramedics came. Questions were asked and photographs taken. The police went off to search for Travis, who shortly afterward turned himself in, and Rasmussen took Jessica to the emergency room.

Once she was cleaned and bandaged and stitched, they returned to her house, outside of which two large pickup trucks were parked and idling. From them emerged two shaven-headed and goateed citizens of the Raider Nation, her uncle, who was half a foot taller than Rasmussen, and her cousin, who was another half-foot taller than that, the two men together weighing more than a quarter-ton.

"Some bad decisions made here tonight," said Jessica with unmistakable defiance in her tone and an air of having had similar conversations with her uncle or father at earlier stages of her life.

"Lot of people making bad decisions!" her uncle shouted quietly.

"I have *no* trouble with what Travis did," the cousin said, almost conversationally. "What I don't understand," he said and stood and pointed his finger at Rasmussen, "is what *you* are doing here."

"You have no trouble with what Travis did," Rasmussen repeated.

"I WOULD HAVE DONE THE SAME THING IN HIS POSITION!"

Rasmussen was very tired, and consequently fearless and persuasive in a way that well-rested decent people can never be. "Well," he said slowly, "I have a lot of trouble with you having no trouble about what Travis did. But I'm really tired so I'm just going to say that I was unhappy and Jessica was unhappy and we shared our unhappiness for a while. I can't recommend it but that's what we did."

This appeared to mollify or confuse the cousin. He dropped his accusing finger and asked if Rasmussen would mind if he and his father talked to Jessica alone.

Rasmussen looked at Jessica. "I owe them an explanation," she said, and smiled.

"All right. I will say goodnight then." And he left, walking slowly to his car and getting in on the passenger's side only after a great deal of weary tugging. There was a great deal of blood on his shirt, but it was the blood of other people, solely, which made him want to stab himself in the heart, ease its terrified guilt with a strong flow of his own blood to where it ought to be, mixing with the others.

TRAVIS SPENT FIVE NIGHTS IN JAIL. He called Jessica once to tell her how sorry he was, but he loved her more than ever, his love knew no bounds whatsoever and it had clouded his reason, he was crazy with it, he was the first or at least the second to admit it, and then he had gotten so drunk and so angry, he didn't think, in conclusion, he also thought he could not allow Rasmussen to remain in her life. That was how he put it, from jail, rather too ominously for comfort: *can't allow him to be in your life.*

When he was released, however, it was to his friend's house he went. After a few drinks to steady his nerve, he went next door and rang the bell. When Rasmussen's wife answered, he introduced himself and asked if he could speak to her about recent events in his life, which had confused and saddened him. Their dogs appeared not to sense evil in him, so she invited him in, and he told her the whole story, as he understood it, from his point of view. When he was done, looking at all the classical music on the shelves in the living room, he cried out that he could not fathom why Rasmussen would even want to go to a Jimmy Buffett concert. The dogs came to attention. Rasmussen's wife said she had nothing to say to him about her estranged husband. She said he, Travis, ought to be ashamed of himself for hitting his wife, and Travis said that he was. Then she asked him to leave, and he did. Rasmussen's wife then sought out Jessica. She had of course long suspected them of adultery, but wanted confirmation, details, and some sense of what her husband might be thinking. Halfway through that conversation, Rasmussen called his wife on her cell phone. Reaching into her bag to shut its ringer off, she inadvertently answered the call. Phone still in purse, Rasmussen thus heard muffled mumbled static-fuzzed bits of dialogue that caused him to shout his wife's name over and over until he heard the phone coming out of the bag and his wife thanking Jessica for her time and honesty, then asking Rasmussen where he was. He said he was at work, and she drove there. Meeting in the parking lot, she rolled down her window and laughed at him and said, "However awful you think your life has been, it's going to get very much worse now." Always pretty when she smiled, her eyes had never flashed more beautifully. She was electrified, dark, ecstatic.

TWO DAYS LATER, Jessica came to Rasmussen's apartment. She was lonely and frightened, and her face was a stitched mess of swollen, garishly colored tissue. Immediately upon the release of Rasmussen's hold on himself, he was assailed by a cold that seemed to occupy his entire body. It was Sunday morning, which meant there was a NASCAR race on television. The race was in Talladega, which was the heart of yet another nation, NASCAR Nation, and featured spectacular crashes caused by the unpredictable aerodynamics of what were essentially family sedans going two hundred miles an hour, bumper to bumper, fender to fender, three and four wide. Talladega always promised a "Big One," a crash of five or ten or even twenty cars at once, and it was at just such a moment, brightly colored race cars barrel-rolling through the air like acrobatic stunt planes, or end-over-end, or slamming into retaining walls, exploding into flames and a thousand pieces, that someone knocked on the door. Wrapped in a blanket, puffy-faced and dribbling snot, Rasmussen opened the door on his wife, who entered and began giving orders, the nature and urgency of which were completely lost on him. She ransacked his desk, opening files and envelopes, tossing office supplies around as if she were in a slapstick comedy, tearing up pieces of paper after only the most cursory glances, and then heard Jessica and the race in the next room.

"*You. Out.*"

Jessica stood. "Wild horses couldn't keep me here."

"*Let's go, Barbie. I mean right now. Get out.*"

Then they were shoving each other out the front door and shouting on the sidewalk.

"FUCKING MY HUSBAND! THAT WAS YOUR GOAL IN LIFE?"

"SOMEBODY HAD TO!"

Jessica retreated to her truck, and Rasmussen's wife returned to the apartment, where she continued her mission to command meaninglessly and destroy randomly. Her eyes flashed like lightning

141

without cease for several hours. At one point she suggested with elaborately ironic politeness (she did not have Rasmussen's gift for sarcasm) that he ought to go down on his knees before her, and beg for forgiveness, and he did, thinking as he wept that she wouldn't be acting like that if she didn't actually love him.

[8]

A LONG AND CONFUSING DARK AGE FELL now over not just the team and the company, but, at least from Rasmussen's perspective, the entire world, as well as the whole of his life, past, present, and future. The couch that had once been merely comfortable he could leave now only with great difficulty, fear, and strong calmatives. He vowed to cease and never again resume the drinking of alcohol, and did in fact stop. He practiced mindfulness to the best of his ability, and attended meetings of Alcoholics Anonymous. His wife called two or three or more times a day, sometimes simply to remind him that she hated him, rather perfunctorily, sometimes to describe with what almost amounted to good humor the depth and character of that hatred, and sometimes, though very rarely, to say that she was in her car and going to drive into a bridge abutment. He was always very glad to talk to her, under any circumstances and conditions, but would cry weakly and beg in a very small voice for her to stop when she said things like *here it comes, this is it, I'm stepping on the gas* and he would hear the engine roar fuzzily through the phone, and then the line go dead. Anita Portolan and Edward Cage had offices on either side of him, and would sometimes come to his glass door to see if he was all right. Rasmussen was convinced that at least one of the four people involved in the broken marriages would die, but was afraid that more than one would die, and told his friends he hoped very much that it would be just the one, him, and that that would assuage the gods he had offended.

But generally speaking, once everybody was at work, the days passed bearably. In fact they went remarkably well—at least from one perspective, on one level of intercourse; the team flourished, nearly doubling in size overnight, and Boatman's credit with Jack the founder and his directors ballooned impressively, allowing him to float just above the heads of the crowd, visible to nearly everyone in what was quickly becoming a teeming city of the plain. He secured two new corner offices for himself and his assistant, and channeled fifty thousand dollars to Willie Masters, whose revolutionary business plan had dwindled to an idea for a book, the outline of which he would fail night after night in the local bar to develop. This flashy line of credit and concomitant appearance of big spending and easy living, however, was in bafflingly direct opposition to the neurotic unease of the team itself. Veins of animosity ran very deep now below a quiet surface of candidly false cordiality. The fault-cracked fields of their work trembled with trapped and seething poisons. Alliances came and went with the same kind of passion and capacity to hurt as they had in high school. Acting skill, whether as a natural gift, as an instinctively appropriate sociological response to threat or opportunity, or as a part of a calculated strategy to either conceal or reveal the truth, was much prized.

Rasmussen felt he was bearing the brunt of this deception and hostility. Gelb, the most austere and unflappable of the ex-reporters, while showering on Jessica many forms of concerned and caring attention and pamphlets from HR on subjects ranging from the purchase of real estate to resources for the battered wife, melodramatically refused to speak to him and in fact never again did. He swore he would never countenance the unspoken accusation with a demand that it be spoken, but it seemed that one or two people in the group had come to believe that it was Rasmussen who'd slapped Jessica around. Livia Barker literally turned up her nose at Rasmussen, but this was just as well, as she'd put a life-size cardboard cutout of Xena the Warrior Princess in her office, making it difficult to talk to her in any circumstances. He accepted the idea that it was because he had behaved like such a grandstander (on bad days) and ombudsman (good days) that he was the target and receptacle of deeper and darker forces, understood dimly that the actor is safe only as long as he is pleasing the crowd, and, furthermore and most importantly, was resolved to work the Twelve Steps with his fellow alcoholics, and to practice meditation and the cultivation of peace whenever he could. So, despite the lurking hatreds, the days were in fact bearable, as suggested above, and the team throve. If it was, as Anita Portolan finally conjectured after a long period of doubt following her rejection of Boatman's offer of a "substantial responsibility" (without of course the concomitant authority—basically an offer to do all the shit work so Boatman could finesse ghostwritten books from a crowd of international jet-setting GIS playboys), a castle, full of free beer built on sand; and if, more importantly, if more mysteriously as well, it was true as she suspected that they were being set up, they were going to be allowed to bloat and wallow and then be punctured and slaughtered, by directors secretly convinced Jack the founder was throwing good money after bad, because he could; if all that was true, nevertheless, Anita reminded Rasmussen, it *is* a castle, and peasants are running in and out of the gate all day long with mock alacrity and devotion to the baron so convincing it was hard to spot the deception much less denounce it.

ONE DAY, RASMUSSEN WAS GETTING HIS HAIR CUT. His stylist cut the hair of many people who worked at Environmental Science and Responsibility—it was the biggest employer in town—and she confirmed his sense that things were changing, mainly, it seemed, for the worse, since change was almost always perceived as something going from bad to worse, around the whole company. The message was similar, too: *We're doing great work, the company seems to be doing very well, but something is wrong, they're not happy for reasons*

144

we can't discern, they are determined to fix something that isn't broken. The jaws of the trap were just beginning to creak, Rasmussen thought. Then his stylist said a friend of hers had recently been hired, and she wondered who Rasmussen's boss was.

"Kyle Boatman."

"*Yes.* He's the one who hired her."

"Really. You're sure?"

"Yes, Kyle Boatman."

"First I've heard of it. Which is odd! Damned odd!" He slipped in and out of an upper-class British accent. "Heretofore, all hiring has occurred not just with the knowledge of the team but also with its approval. What's your friend like?"

"Tough, practical, loyal."

"You recommend her highly, then. Just between you and me."

The rhythm of her clipping altered slightly. "Yes, she's wonderful."

It was Boatman's master stroke. His team was both successful in a way that couldn't be proven, and unhappy in ways that couldn't be articulated. He could not control his team, but their work had provided him with carte blanche and a blank check to play with. He could move on the strength of the team's "accomplishments" while appearing to take responsibility for the apparent anarchy of its operation simply by admitting publicly what he'd privately sobbed to Anita—the job was too much for him—and relinquishing his command, or at least the part of it that he didn't care for. The tears were now even closer to the truth.

Boatman fired himself. He went around with a grin both boyish and sheepish and told (select members of) the team that he was doing so because, frankly and modestly, he wasn't doing a very good job. The team (select members of) was filled with foreboding, as they wanted nothing more, most of them, than to be left alone to do the kind of work they were good at, and feared the coming of a drill sergeant or efficiency expert or arrogant ninny or whoever it was they had up their sleeves, the scoundrels who ran the company and their lackeys. *Don't worry,* said Boatman, losing some of the boyishness and sheepishness of the grin as well as the modesty and candor of the confession. *I'll still be here. I'm just going to concentrate on what I do best.* Rasmussen wrote an e-mail message to him saying with friendly diplomacy that a mutual friend had more or less spoiled his surprise, but that she had recommended her friend very highly, a recommendation that Rasmussen took very seriously and that made him consequently very eager to meet and begin to work with June Hoover. In the course of replying, Boatman, displaying the same kind of maladroit savvy that had driven him to give Anita Portolan's ID tag to his wife, included a back-and-forth between Boatman and Hoover.

"*How much does he know?*" she'd wondered.

"*Don't worry,*" he reassured her.

Rasmussen was so stunned, could so little credit what he most certainly had read, that he instinctively withdrew into secrecy, and was slow—perhaps too slow, though even hindsight suggested no recourse—to reveal what he appeared to know, even to Anita, who knew her way around the company, and might conceivably have thought of something to do, to halt or at least divert the juggernaut.

JUNE E. HOOVER ARRIVED QUIETLY during the lunch hour of a day in the middle of the next week. No one expected her, and she behaved as courteously as if she were simply a friend of Boatman's—or rather, his mother—and only passing through. A round of interviews was scheduled, but to what purpose nobody on the team quite knew. Nobody knew anything about her, nobody knew what her position and title would be, nobody knew what kind of responsibilities she would have, and, finally, nobody knew the nature or extent of either the responsibility or the authority that had, evidently, been given her.

She presented herself as an ambitious kindergarten teacher and revealed nothing of herself in conversation. She was very much a machine of the gods, Rasmussen suggested, asking his friends if he might be forgiven for turning the phrase around, raised up and set in place by a kind of invisible corporate crane to the large-gestured wailing and moaning of the chorus, who did not have the slightest idea what to say to her otherwise. In the course of the very awkward interviews, she told the team she was there to help them be successful. She particularly wanted to nurture their vision and support their creativity. Because most of what the team now produced was books, they were going to call themselves a press, the managing editor of which she would be, and Kyle Boatman its publisher. Reams of letterhead with this new information had already been purchased.

"You are a very important member of this team," she said to Rasmussen, rising at the conclusion of their meeting.

"*Oh please,*" laughed Rasmussen, pretending that she was flattering him and that flattery, while much appreciated, would really get her nowhere because his integrity was too unrelenting.

"I'm counting on you," she confided.

"You are?" asked Rasmussen, letting the ambiguity fall with equal emphasis on both syllables of his magnificently cloaked stranger at the well.

"Yes," said Junie (call me that) Hoover, softly and sincerely. "I am."

"Okay," said Rasmussen. "But who are you?"

Though reports of a veiled imperiousness animating every grandmotherly cookie-bearing movement of her eyes came in immediately from all corners of the team, it was Edward Cage and the Russians who had the first constructive criticisms to voice. Cage, gathering anecdotal material, noted what he thought was a recurring phenomenon: a lack of interest in anything specific that team members might try to say about the operation of the team. He believed that was because she already knew everything she needed to know, or rather, believed it so because she had heard all about it, everybody's sordid life story, with special attention to how they contributed to the great pain in Boatman's neck that was his team's success—she had heard it from the lips of a god. She has not been set down amongst us, said Cage, to *help* us. She is here to protect Kyle Boatman *from* us. She is Boatman's man. Worse: she is Boatman's mom.

Images from documentary films about wildlife and natural systems flashed through Rasmussen's mind: the mother bird pretending to have a broken wing as she limps histrionically away from the nest, the mommy rhino knocking a Land Rover on its side, images from children's books both good and bad of little animals curled up snugly against larger animals wearing lipstick or milkmaid caps to distinguish their sex, mothers in movies, and, finally, more complicatedly, his own mother. But with this crucial, creepy difference: as all these mothers went through their paces, he saw the clever child smirkingly directing every last little bit of heartwarming and violent nonsense.

The Russians sighed and shrugged their shoulders. Rasmussen went outside with them to smuk cigarette, and they laughed at his naiveté when he said he couldn't believe it but the team clearly didn't matter, the people who actually did the work didn't matter, they never had, it was the same old story, it had never been about doing good work, it was about back-stabbing deceit and kicking people in the teeth who were on the rung just below you, and so on. The Russians smukked cigarette silently, sneering in that peculiar Russian way around the glowing cherries. Yes it was true, they didn't matter. Their job was to obey. Did Rasmussen think he was Chekhov? An esteemed member of the intelligentsia? No, he was not. Walter, they cried to him, tapping him on the breastbone and breaking his personal space in other ways as well, belly to belly, nose in ear, Walter you are huplissly stupid if you think this! There were fourteen ranks in the czar's civil service and they were in the fourteenth rank. They were clerks, above only the peasants, and their rank entitled them to one courtesy and one courtesy only: they could go to the police and complain if their superiors beat them.

"*Above* peasants."

"*Da.* One step."

Both Russians placed their forefingers almost on the tip of Rasmussen's nose.

But when Rasmussen told Anita Portolan what the Russians had said, she didn't looked convinced. She felt there was more to it than that. Something fishy. They left her office and looked down the hallway at Boatman's office, where he and Junie could be seen conferring at a small table.

"Look at their body language," said Anita.

"Oh my god," said Rasmussen. "They're in love."

"*She* is in love. *He* is encouraging her to *think* so."

It turned out that she was encouraging him to think that he was encouraging her to think that they were in love—she was in love with *powerful* people *much* higher up—but that didn't become clear until many months later.

SEVERAL EVENTS OCCURRED almost simultaneously now. Edward Cage learned that his old house underneath the freeway was, for a freakish moment in the freakish moment that is Southern California, worth more than four times what he paid for it a few years earlier. Emboldened by the thought, tragically fleeting, that he was suddenly independently wealthy, he stepped up the frequency of his "Letters to the Founder," and, overcome by his eloquence and the candor that only great wealth can provide, intensified the quality of the invective as well. He called his old friend Jack "my old friend Jack," and explained that their ancient loyalty not only allowed but demanded that he tell Jack frankly what an idiot and asshole he had become in the last couple years, how mean-spirited and gratuitous his new policies seemed to be, how incompetent and nasty his new managers were proving to be. For these efforts, Cage was, in a corporate way, arrested, tried secretly, and condemned to new regulations controlling his work habits and production that not even the illegal immigrants cleaning the bathrooms had to endure. He came away from his trial with stories of how the very shapes of the faces of his judges had been distorted by their rage. *You say you thought you were doing the right thing, Edward? Well, well, we will leave it to you to reconcile that righteousness with your punishment. Don't take it too hard, though. You had a pretty easy time there for a few years, didn't you? Didn't you? DIDN'T YOU!* Anita Portolan, that same weekend, was stopped at the border because she was a Canadian with the wrong papers (they were actually the right ones, and in superb order), denied entrance to the United States, and flown back to Toronto, whence she struggled to return to her job, home, and fiancé for more than two weeks. Rasmussen's wife returned from a month of travel around the country to announce her determination to proceed with the divorce, including now custody of their two dogs, and news not just from in-laws and her friends but also Rasmussen's friends, some of the oldest and best, that they had known all along he was one of the most terrific assholes ever produced on earth. Once such denunciation came from a very old and very dear friend and covered not just the conduct of his marriage but his entire life, suggesting that he was actually hated by his parents and brother, too. This did not ring true—the ferocity and poison of it took him completely by surprise and even after he'd mulled it over it seemed directed at some other person, a person he quite clearly did not know, but as per AA he knew there were no steps calling for the defense of the self. He must make a thorough search of his soul, take a moral inventory, confess his sins, beg forgiveness, and make amends where he could. On the other hand, one thing the wisdom systems of the world have in common is the idea that one should not over-think. The less thinking, the better off one is, generally speaking. The thought of relinquishment on that scale seemed to fill Rasmussen with oxygen, and he wept with joy, tears being once again very close to the truth. Meekly, but feeling wondrously strong, he accepted his wife's hatred without a peep, and wrote to his friend asking forgiveness. He even went so far as to request a moment of Boatman's time, and apologized for the bad blood that had coursed between them too often, the misunderstandings and unfortunate events that had rocked the team's little boat. He said he was Boatman's man in the end, and would do everything in his power to make the team's future as promisingly bright as his own now apparently promised to be.

Boatman was unmoved. He was not on the same page of recovery. He stared at Rasmussen with uncharacteristic anger and agreed that Rasmussen had a lot to answer for. The conversation was definitely not going according to the script, but Rasmussen merely nodded. Then he said in a warm and friendly tone that he wasn't sure what Boatman was talking about. Boatman then listed a number of episodes in which Rasmussen had played what he thought was the part of ombudsman (his favorite word around the office), but that Boatman believed to show once and for all that Rasmussen was the source of all evil on the team. That, strikingly, in a corporate office environment, was precisely the phrase employed: *source of all evil*. Again thinking that it simply didn't ring true, and again thinking that it simply wouldn't do to think too much about it, Rasmussen retired from the scene. Boatman, sensing vulnerability (Cage had been humiliated and his naggingly meticulous ethical badgerings silenced at least temporarily—and the confusingly alluring Anita was out of the picture too, and could not for the moment make him feel like an idiot and lovesick pupil), perhaps just working out some dimly understood neurotic need of his own, as well as being caught up in the heady rush of having someone around to (apparently) adore him and do his bidding unquestioningly (wrap

this noose around my neck, yes, that's right, now hang me), wrote
to Junie Hoover that it was time to bring Rasmussen to heel. And
so it came to pass that Junie, on the job officially less than a week
and possessed of no experience in writing, editing, publishing, or
geographic information systems (that wasn't what she was hired
for, you fucking *fool*, Rasmussen thought he heard someone whis-
pering *she was hired to get rid of the weirdos*), decided to critique
Rasmussen's work as a means of introducing herself—not just to
him, of course, but to the undisciplined and narcissistic team as a
complete and sentient thing itself.

Back cover copy for a book of case studies dealing with the
design and development of geodatabases was chosen as the issue. Via
e-mail, but no more than four doors away from him, Junie said she
wanted Rasmussen to *revisit* it. It felt first-draftish, and she knew he
knew that, and knew also that he could do better. So, revisit it! What
could be more charming? *A visit! A revisit! Coffee? Pastry?* Rasmussen
replied that he knew nothing of the kind. He said he would be happy
to revise the copy if Junie had some compelling criticism, but the mid-
dleman meddling, devoid of substance, would not fly with him. He
suggested, in a spirit of party-giving, that Junie *visit* the back covers
of the books they had already published, which featured some of the
best back cover copy anyone could hope for. (That was, he instantly
regretted, how he put it. But there it was, not only as unwithdrawable
as blurted speech—electronically documented too!) Junie replied that
she wanted to talk about the issues he was raising. Rasmussen replied that not only had he written most of the back cover copy for
most of the company's books, and not only had he reviewed books
for the *New York Times,* the *Boston Globe,* the *Washington Post,* the
Philadelphia Inquirer, the *Chicago Tribune,* the *Los Angeles Times,* the
San Francisco Chronicle, and *The Nation,* he was once a publicist for
a large independent bookstore and *wrote promotional copy for exactly
one thousand books in the space of five fucking years.* He realized only
just then that he had lost his temper.

Seeking to deflate the tension that was building steadily around them by making light of it, he apologized and suggested a quick face-to-face. In his office, above the whiteboard, hung the toy spear. He took it, wobbling in its rubbery armature, to the threshold of Junie's office. He wagged his eyebrows à la Groucho Marx and asked Junie if she thought he was going to need it during their conversation. It was a gamble, he was quite clear that he might simply look stupid, but Junie laughed; maybe she was the good person his stylist believed her to be after all. Relieved and confident, Rasmussen sat down.

They conducted a frank and reasonable discussion and parted with optimism and warm goodwill. Rasmussen was in fact so moved by the success of the talk that he rushed home to get a copy of a chapbook of travel essays written by him and his wife a few years earlier, just before their marriage began to go wrong. It was published by a very small press and sold fewer than a hundred copies, mostly to friends and family, but it was a beautiful book, and Rasmussen inscribed it *To June Hoover, with an open heart and an open mind, Walter Rasmussen.*

The weekend passed with Rasmussen contentedly painting the eaves of the house in which he no longer lived and would soon lose. A new week commenced. Bright and early Monday morning he took a call from Human Resources: small matter needed to be discussed, could he accommodate them more or less immediately? On the patio beneath the palm trees next to the koi pond, where once Travis had inexpertly spied on Jessica, Human Resources asked him if it was true that he had brought a weapon to a meeting and threatened June Hoover with it.

WITH NEITHER CAGE'S PERSUASIVE GOOD SENSE nor Anita's political savvy to restrain or guide or comfort him, Rasmussen confronted Boatman and Junie in the office's common area, and used a loud, sarcastic tone of voice to describe the situation.

"What have you two been reading?" he wanted to know. *"Machiavelli for Dummies?"*

"Really now," whispered Junie, "do I look Machiavellian to you?"

"Oh for CHRIST'S SAKE!" shouted Rasmussen.

"What do you mean, Machiavellian?" asked Boatman in a businesslike manner.

"Behavior marked by cunning, duplicitousness, or bad faith," said Rasmussen.

"Oh come off it, mate," chortled Boatman to Junie's wink. "It's behavior marked by straightforward good faith and sound business principles. The big difference here today is that you don't have your co-conspirators to back you up. You have to face—"

"CO-CONSPIRATORS!" Rasmussen exploded. "WHAT THE FUCK ARE YOU *TALKING* ABOUT?"

"Darn't think we haven't noticed all the animated conversations behind closed doors that you and Cage and Anita have been having," said Boatman seriously. "Closed doors send the wrong signal. Your peers don't like it. This isn't a closed door kind of place."

Rasmussen's jaw dropped and he literally gaped. "You have *got* to be kidding me."

"This is no joking matter!" said Boatman with sudden vehemence.

Rasmussen sighed deeply and sadly, having come back to himself at just that moment and recovered his dignity. He leaned forward in his chair and said he was sorry it had come to this, sorry that he was acting in this ungentlemanly, unsatisfactory, and unproductive way, just plain sorry that—at which point Boatman leapt up, grabbed him by the hand, and slapped his wrist.

"THAT'S WHAT WE WANTED YOU TO SAY IN THE FIRST PLACE!"

Rasmussen looked slowly back and forth between Hoover and Boatman. "That's what you wanted me to say in the first place."

"Yes!"

"This was a what, a proactive team-building exercise designed specifically to . . . to *humble me?*"

"That's not how we want to put it," cooed Junie.

"And just to make sure I've been properly humbled," said Rasmussen, standing and heading for the door, "you *struck* me."

"I didn't strike you, mate. If I'd've struck you, you'd've known it." Boatman's tone of voice and the look in his eye had noticeably changed. "That was a love tap, mate," he said, actually smiling. He could not quite, however, conceal the nervous anxiety he had caused to well in his stomach: even light remonstrances, if they were physical, were . . . were not really acceptable. Unless . . . unless you were clearly joking with a friend . . . no . . .? Very clearly . . .?

Rasmussen stood in the doorway. He was trembling but not sure if it was visible agitation or the slow bringing to boil of adrenaline in his veins. His shoulders were hunched and his face was hot. He feared he might be on the edge of serious convulsion or apoplexy, because despite the good progress down the road of recovery, it was hard not to notice how poorly he was feeling. His wrist, which had actually been grasped and restrained and struck, was burning. He was familiar enough with this condition to be afraid of himself, of what he might do, and could feel panic building as his body tried to work out if it was to flee or not, and if not flee, then fight or not, and if fight, how strenuously and to what end? His breath was coming shorter and harder the longer he stood there, one second, two seconds, three seconds, and he was able to see less and less of the room. He made out Boatman's grin floating in the air like the Cheshire cat's. June Hoover had insisted she was frightened when he appeared with the toy spear, and while she could not conceivably have been, unless her susceptibility to fear was pathological, she most certainly was now, whether Rasmussen's rage was visible or not.

Then, in a room completely empty save a nervous toothy smile, a soft female voice, pitched somewhere between loving remonstrance and professional sympathy, asked Rasmussen to imagine how his wife or mother or sister would have felt if they had been confronted in *their* offices by a man with a spear.

It was such a ridiculous idea that for a moment Rasmussen wondered if it had been attempted for the sake of comic relief, somewhat in the spirit of the spear itself. He stared at the space where the voice came from until he could see Junie Hoover, as sincere-seeming as the day was long, and he was able to snort with derision and turn away and leave the office.

FINALLY, LATE THAT NIGHT, or rather very early the next morning, San Bernardino County Search and Rescue was called to find a hiker lost on the far side of the mountains that protected the valley from the high desert. On an otherwise empty road, they collided with a drunken methedrine addict who had strayed from his lane: westbound, he was on the shoulder of the eastbound lane, going about a hundred. Three people in the Search and Rescue SUV were killed, two of them from Environmental Science and Responsibility, and Travis. Rasmussen's neighbor was alive but appeared to be paralyzed. The drunken meth addict really had no idea what had happened. The company and the city both mourned the loss. The flag at city hall was flown at half-mast for three days, and a large public memorial service was held. Rasmussen wanted to attend the memorial, but friends assured him he was not thinking clearly, and should not attend.

[9]

ANITA PORTOLAN RETURNED to the United States of America with a new perspective—not just on international relations, which was to be expected given the war on terror, but on how things were going generally with capitalism. She had been trying to read what business school graduates were reading, the more popular and read-able essays on management, and it turned out, she told Rasmussen, to be the same old shit: uniformity of product, minimal production costs, and market predictability. Rasmussen, in the course of a life of playwriting, bookselling, arts reviewing, and repeated failure to be extraordinary and unconstrained by reality in his pursuit of beauty and truth, had seen the learned playboys of publishing become Wal-Mart suppliers, had seen the festering corpse of Broadway reani-mated by Mouseketeers running a protection racket, and philosophy become marketing, and so could think that he had fallen asleep only because he worked for a software manufacturer who was so success-ful he could run a press as he might a kennel of Lhasa apsos, as pets, because he liked the breed. We didn't have to make a profit, he told Anita, so we were free to be ridiculous.

"We published a couple good books," Anita reminded him.

"They can't take that away from us," Rasmussen agreed.

"Your days are numbered, though. You know that, don't you?"

"I see that they are numbered. I may choose not to accept the figure."

"What are you going to do?"

"I don't know."

"Content will be provided by offshore content providers and coded by trained coders so that it can be poured without spilling into a funnel on one side of our designers' computers, which will poop books out the other side. From a nozzle. They will be soft at first, but will harden into books." Anita began to cry and laugh at the same time in a kind of competition. "Oh, they hate me, they hate me, they just fucking *hate* me, Walter! They know I know how to do what they do, and how long it takes to do it, and they will never ever forgive me." She stopped suddenly and covered her mouth. Her eyes widened. "No," she said, "you know what it is? I am *The Woman Who Knew Too Much*. I am the only loose end of the perfect crime. They are going to have to kill me."

The next morning, a meeting of the entire group was called. The theme was "Creative Resources and Team Building." After introductory remarks and a nod from Hoover, the heretofore thoroughly estimable Satyavati Swenson cleared her throat and said she had felt excluded and slighted in the production of the team's last big effort, a collection of historical maps, selected from a large and well-known personal holding in San Francisco, digitally transformed and in provocative and entertaining ways enhanced by geographic information systems software. Because cartography and manipulation of the GIS software constituted 99 percent of the book's design elements, Anita Portolan had perforce been the book's designer, as well as its writer and editor and project manager. But Satyavati, speaking for the rest of the designers, too, said she had not been able to participate in any meaningful and creative way, and consequently had not been allowed to enjoy any of the acclaim that the book was eliciting, not just in cartographic or GIS libraries but broadly in the trade. It was a dramatic restating of a long-standing complaint, and June Hoover had seized on it just as she had on Rasmussen's spear. When Anita came to her office privately to protest, Hoover sweetly acknowledged the rock and the hard place Anita found herself between, and cooed soothingly over the brilliance of the book. Then she turned to Anita's current project, a cartography textbook. It seemed to be taking longer than expected, and the designer's schedules were in jeopardy of being jostled. Hoover asked Anita therefore to provide her with a daily accounting of her progress. When Anita moved to another, distant part of the company, no one even said good-bye, and Rasmussen's hatred for his former friends deepened dangerously.

IT WAS ALL SO CHILDISH, so petty. Rasmussen sat in his office and brooded. Certainly he wasn't feeling well: the dizzy spells had settled in at a low level but high frequency—he was more or less always "lightheaded"—his face was hot and dark red at times that had no correspondence with rage or frustration, he often ran temperatures of 100 and was so exhausted that breathing seemed a chore—and, as a kind of finishing flourish to every bout of consciousness, he would astound and repel himself with his achievements on the toilet. But surely there was something more going on than disordered biochemistry. He was ashamed of himself. He knew the furnace in his brain—not the organ but the thinking—ran on fear, but what he was afraid of he could not say. Was he afraid to say? It was possible. Was he afraid to know? That was much more likely. If he knew, he would say so. He was not so afraid that he could not say what he knew. But could he know? Did he know? He could know if he wanted to, but he was afraid to know. Which meant he knew but was afraid to say. He was a coward of the worst sort: he could not face himself. It made just enough sense to sicken him, to make him feel like someone had a fist in his guts and was squeezing his diaphragm. Was he afraid of losing his job? It was contemptible to think so, and yet . . . had he not just said it? By saying it did he now not know it? Was his job contemptible, and his fearlessness demonstrated by his contempt for it? Or was he contemptible and his fear demonstrated by that very same contempt. Yes, it was certainly all childish and petty—but was not the childish negotiation of petty grievance the primary mode of behavior in the United States of America? Was it not the fundamental means of social and political intercourse? Were not the winners, the rulers, simply men and women who had grown up enough to manage the playground? Were not the losers and the ruled those who simply charged about the playground performing fuming little dramas—*He said this and I said that and then he said something else and I smashed him to the ground*—about the unfairness of life and the extraordinariness of the stories they had to tell?

Willie Masters was in the habit of telephoning both Boatman and Rasmussen regularly, ostensibly with updates on the progress of his book—he was continuing his research and had, as well, rearranged his bookshelves to accommodate what would soon be a staggering mass of it, a deft organization that would make drafting chapters simply a matter of assimilating one pile after another—but in truth in the hope of getting (a) more money from Boatman, and (b) Rasmussen to do the final, actual writing, after transcription and synthesis of hundreds of hours of phoned monologues. And so it was that Masters called Rasmussen in the middle of his brooding and heard, once he was persuaded to stop talking, a reckless confession of confusion and contrition.

"Son of Erasmus," intoned Masters, "this is the collapse of the consciousness into sensitivity. I'll say it again: *collapse of the consciousness into sensitivity.*"

"What is that," asked Rasmussen, "Emerson?"

"HA HA HA HA HA HA HA! Emerson! HA HA HA HA HA HA HA! *Emerson?* HA HA HA HA HA HA HA! You slay me, Erasmus, you surely do! No, no, son, that's a psychologist name of Bennett. Listen to me now. The interval between the finitude of specifiable roles and the transfinitude of the play of initiative—are you with me, son? I know you can handle this stuff, Walter, so listen close. That fucking interval can be regarded as immense or infinitesimal. *It is the step from quantity to quality.* When the two realms 'collapse' into one, we have the 'ordinary state' of discourse. We call this state 'degenerate'—HA HA HA HA, and that goes especially for you, Walter my son!—in the technical sense of reducing multivalue to either/or choices. Bennett speaks of this in terms of the collapse of consciousness into sensitivity, where 'consciousness' refers to the transfinite (or 'cosmic') and 'sensitivity' to the finite (or vital) aspects of our awareness."

"Willie, that makes no sense to me at all."

"You can look it up and read it for yourself. The writer's name is Bennett and the URL is www.structuresofmeaning.com."

"I don't want to look it up. I want you to talk to me in plain English."

"All right, how's this: *A mind out of control will do more harm than two angry men engaged in combat.*"

"*That's* Emerson."

"HA HA HA HA HA HA HA!"

"It's *not* Emerson."

"That's the Enlightened One! The monk Gautama! Siddhartha! HA HA HA HA HA HA HA! That's the Buddha himself talkin', son!"

Masters then returned to Bennett and the collapse of the consciousness into sensitivity, because he was quite sure Rasmussen would understand him in the end, and would reap great benefits from that understanding. After a while he began to speak explicitly of Kyle Boatman, how Rasmussen was failing to understand and appreciate him and how understanding and appreciating Kyle Boatman would bring his consciousness back from its collapse into sensitivity. He would, turning to Maslow, fully realize himself. He would, returning to the Buddha, cease to suffer. He would, referring to Rasmussen's very own words, no longer be afraid.

"By understanding and appreciating Kyle Boatman."

"He's a Jungian hero."

"Kyle Boatman is a Jungian hero."

"That's right."

"Well I guess I don't have a very good grasp of what makes a Jungian hero a Jungian hero, but I would say the very last thing Kyle Boatman is is a hero, Jungian or otherwise."

"He has repeatedly saved your life, son."

"Saved my life?"

"That's right."

"You have got to be kidding me."

"No joke, Walter. He's been looking out for you."

"He's done no such thing."

"When you were going through your bad spell."

"He knows next to nothing about my bad spell."

"He knows enough."

161

"When was it, for starters? When I was producing all those goddamn books for him? When he thought so highly of me he introduced me to his secret weapon—you? Or is it now? Now is what I would call a bad spell but I do not see Kyle fucking Boatman looking out for anybody but himself!"

"He was deeply troubled when you—"

"Let me tell you a completely ordinary and superficially not very interesting story about two men looking out for each other. It's actually kind of boring, but it illustrates something about the human character that I think you will find of value. There's these two guys, right? One's the boss and the other guy is an employee he's looking out for, who's keeping weird hours and missing meetings and stuff like that. This guy, the troubled one, gets up early one morning to catch a flight to Washington, D.C., and faints. He's alarmed by this sudden departure of much-needed consciousness. He decides to miss the flight, skip the meeting in D.C., and just say to his boss, look man, I fainted, I don't think I want to fly across the country, but you know, I am embarrassed to admit that I fainted, it sounds like something women used to do in the movies when they received a shock or saw a mouse, you know what I mean, boss, so, you know, *don't tell anybody I fainted, okay?* And the boss says, sure, sure, kid, not to worry, I'm looking out for you. Great, says the employee, because I don't know why I fainted, and I would prefer not to give, you know, people a chance to *speculate*. No worries, mate, says the boss again. Are you still with me, Willie? Because this is where the punch line to this boring little tale of hurt feelings and misunderstanding comes in. *The boss tells no one anything about what has happened.* But that's what the employee wanted, right? Well, not quite. He wanted 'people in the office' not to know, so they might be forestalled, you see, in their capacity to gossip about someone who maybe had been talked about too much—maybe for reasons that were his own damn fault, and maybe not. But did the employee not want his superiors to know? If that were so, Willie, why would he have told his boss? Did he not want the important person he was meeting to be apprised of his illness? Did he want to stand this guy up and have him squawk to his boss's boss about being stood up by some twerp who was supposed to be glorifying his holy name? Why would he want that? Why would he want to be hauled into his boss's boss's office and hollered at when he had a perfectly good excuse and had already logged that excuse *with his boss?* And finally, Willie, why would the boss, when he saw that his employee was going to get his ass handed to him *and* be gossiped about, when the very things he said he was going to ward off were imminent, why would the boss say to the employee, sorry, I misunderstood, when you said *don't tell anyone* I thought you meant *don't tell anyone.* I see now that I was absurd to think such a thing, but can you cover me? Can you take this hit yourself? There won't be any major repercussions. You go in and talk to my boss and just take the hit and he will understand. He's been through, just between you and me, mate, he's been through a lot and knows all about the Twelve Steps. *He will understand,* Willie. I know those words are echoing and colliding in your big mighty brain. I know you are as offended as I am by the idea that the truth is a lie and the lie is the truth—"

"Aw, Walter man, come on."

"*During my bad spell he actively undermined me. He lied and he cheated and he stole. He took no responsibility whatsoever for his actions. He pitted people against each other, telling one person one thing, and another another. He ignored my best work, gave my authors to other editors, dumped shit work on me—*"

"That's not how he sees it, Walter."

"He was instinctively—no, you listen to me now, Willie, goddammit, I know you can follow this, he was instinctively working against understanding, not because he's *bad*, Willie, or because he's *stupid*, Willie, but *because that is how you succeed in business.*"

"While lesser minds were confused he was working at very great under—"

"AND NOW HE'S GOT A FUCKING PIT BULL TO DO IT ALL FOR HIM!"

"He saw someone who was talented but very erratic in his work habits. He—"

"I AM HIS MOST PRODUCTIVE EDITOR! EVEN DURING MY BAD SPELL WHEN I AM DYING!"

"He saw someone coming off the rails, Walter—"

"Saw? Saw? I'm coming off the rails NOW."

"—who was in danger of taking everybody else along with him."

"That is the most amusingly deluded idea I think I have ever heard."

"He believes in you, Walter. He cares for you. He knows your secret, Walter. He knows how special you think you are, and here's the kicker, son, here's the best part: *He thinks you're special too.*"

[10]

EARLY THE NEXT MORNING, Boatman entered Rasmussen's office with an article that he thought Rasmussen might find interesting. He handed it over as if slapping an opponent with a glove. Almost without prelude they were shouting at each other. Boatman attempted to close the door and Rasmussen threw it back open, announcing that from now on there would be no more secrets, no more deceit, no more saying one thing to one person and another to another, no more backstabbing. They then fell to a reckless and confused examination and comparison of evil deeds, Boatman insisting that Rasmussen has created an atmosphere of strife and suspicion because he was unstable and liable to go to pieces at any moment, making people edgy, Rasmussen countering that while it was undeniably true that his (Rasmussen's) own personal hellfire had threatened to blacken the marshmallows of his friends and colleagues, it was the boss and his selfishness and insecurity whence all miscarriages of justice, trust, and compassion flowed.

They became quiet and abusive for several minutes. Then Rasmussen ran into the common area, returning with a box full of foam core-backed reproductions of all their book covers and event posters and project awards and tossed one after another on the floor, saying *I did this, I did this, I did this, I did this, I did this and this and this and this this this this*—at which Boatman laughed angrily and said, "I'm not the one who fucked Jessica!"

Rasmussen was stopped cold with astonishment. He was so confounded by the idea that he had to shake his head to clear it. He pretended he could not believe what he just heard, putting hand to ear.

"You think that didn't upset people?" demanded Boatman superciliously.

"Most of them had no idea."

"*They all knew.*"

"YOU knew, Kyle, and that is about fucking IT."

"EVERYBODY KNEW!"

"That I was the bad dragon who took the princess away from her fairy kingdom?"

"You think that didn't upset—"

"The fair and beloved virgin taken from her—"

"Are you going to stand there and tell me—"

"*What, you think she had nothing to do with it?* YOU'VE FUCKING CANONIZED HER but me—"

"SOMEONE HAD TO LOOK OUT FOR THE WOMEN AROUND HERE!"

"—but me, no, me, I'm the SCUM OF THE FUCKING EARTH!"

At this, Boatman shrugged. And it was the shrug, the casually dismissive shrugging off of this intimation, this faint ringing that for once did not sound false, that did it. Rasmussen said he saw what it was, he suddenly understood, he got it: he had done what Boatman had wanted desperately to do, and Boatman would never forgive him. He shook his head and looked up just as Boatman snapped, stepping back onto the threshold of the office and shrieking that he did not have to have sex outside his marriage, he had a good marriage and sex outside marriage was bad bad *bad*. Then he threw the pen he'd had in his hand at Rasmussen.

It sailed past Rasmussen's head and clattered against the window. Had it struck him, the whole sorry mess would have been over, but it did not. Rasmussen asked Boatman after a very long moment of silence if he'd thrown something at him. Boatman said no, no, he hadn't thrown it *at* him, man. Rasmussen said he was quite sure that Boatman had done exactly that. *No*, pled Boatman. *Come on, man.* His eyes were red and his voice cracked in his suddenly dry mouth. Rasmussen's eyes, too, were filled with tears. The two men stood facing each other but with eyes cast down, breathing heavily, struggling not to sob, very close to the truth, but not close enough.

CONDITIONS REMAINED AT THIS hysterically intense level, astonishingly, exhaustingly, for several months. Rasmussen edited a long and ambitious, closely reasoned, theoretically controversial, and lovingly detailed book about the history of maps and medicine, called *Cartographies of Disease*. Its author was learned, persuasive, and witty. He was a pleasure to work with, and did not hesitate to say the feeling was mutual. The work was so satisfying that Rasmussen was able to convince himself that all was well. He worked mostly at night and on the weekends, and worked as often as he could at home, as well, believing that what was out of sight was out of mind. He was able to resist the advice of co-workers from other parts of the company who had heard about the spear setup, the wrist-slapping, the pen-throwing, to go to Human Resources, likening Human Resources to the gestapo and swearing he would die before he cooperated with such pigs. The truth was that he did

not want to hurt Kyle Boatman. He did not understand why he felt
that way, when everything he thought he knew about himself suggested revenge so bloodthirsty as to be criminally psychotic, but that
was inescapably how he felt. He hated Boatman, loathed Boatman—
Hoover was so despicable she didn't register on the ordinary scale—
but he refused to hurt Kyle Boatman. Somewhat in the same way he
had not wanted to fight Travis.

He handed *Cartographies of Disease* off to Satyavati.

The next day the author phoned to say he needed to make a
very important revision and extension of a crucial chapter. Rasmussen
agreed that it was important and told Satyavati he would need a few
more days, possibly as much as a week. Her face was a blank mask
when she nodded. An hour later, Junie Hoover called him into her
office. Sati, she said with soft reproof, was upset, and rightly so, at
having such a monkey wrench thrown in her works.

"I understand it's inconvenient," said Rasmussen, "and I'm
sorry—"

"She says you didn't even apologize." Hoover made a face.

"I understand it's inconvenient, and I'm sorry that it's so, but
really we have no choice. The author feels it would be grave mistake
to publish the book as it is right now."

"That's not what you thought yesterday."

"That's right. We changed our minds. A press that can't accommodate the unpredictability of creative endeavor doesn't deserve
to publish a book as good as this one."

"Really, Walter, stop and think. It's a matter of the Golden Rule,
isn't it? How would you like it if Sati did something similar to you?"

"If what I was doing was of secondary importance, if what
I was doing was in the service of what she was doing, I would accept the inconvenience for what it was and do whatever I had to
do to help."

"We depend on our designers to produce our books, Walter.
We'd be lost without them. It's not fair of you to dismiss their hard

work as being of secondary importance. And I think you know that. But what's done is done. We would have to delay production anyway, because you haven't properly prepared the manuscript."

"In what way have I not properly prepared the manuscript?"

"Our design templates call for all headings to be in lowercase letters."

"The designers have a button they can press to fix that."

"Yes, but it's your job to prepare the manuscript. Asking them to do part of your job, too, when they're already understaffed, well, come on now, Walter, that's not very fair of you, either, is it."

"It's not my job. I edit. They produce."

"Our template also calls for single spaces between sentences, not two, as you have allowed."

"They've got a button for that."

"I'd like you to do that."

Rasmussen did some quick arithmetic. "At five seconds per operation, that would take me about half a year. If I got really good at it, and could cut my time per operation in half, we're still talking about several months. As little as you pay me, you could pay a high schooler working after classes even less."

"What a good idea."

"That's it." Rasmussen stood up. He was afraid of something else more than he was afraid of losing his job, something he could not name but that reduced him to a quivering, leaden-tongued, stiff-legged Rumpelstiltskin-like caricature of himself. "I quit." He tossed his ID and keycards across the table. Then he fluttered his fingers in farewell.

THE SUDDEN AND PRECIPITOUS LOSS of income complicated and in some ways sharpened the symptoms of unwellness he was trying to ignore: someone said his eyes were beginning to bug out a bit, and maybe his thyroid was out of whack, but he stayed firm, for no apparent reason, in rejecting the idea of seeing his doctor. Quitting his job also complicated, naturally, the divorce. One feature of the separation, however, was nonnegotiable, and that was that the dogs should stay in their home with his wife, and with this Rasmussen was in complete agreement. Under no circumstances would he take them from their home. Under no circumstances would he subject his wife to that loneliness and grief. He walked them every day, sometimes twice a day, and stayed with them when she was out of town. Habit fixed the walks in the midmorning or at dusk. One very hot and smoggy day in the middle of summer, however, discouraged exercise. Rasmussen promised his dogs they would walk later that night, when the air would be at least cleaner, if not much cooler. Around midnight, he went outside and figured it was now or never. He leashed the dogs, and they walked down the driveway and started up the street. When they drew abreast of his erstwhile neighbor's garage, the motion detector that Travis had connected to the yard lights triggered the lights, and Rasmussen froze. He held his hand up against the glare. They were like two great burning eyes, two portals into heaven or hell, he could not say which, it seemed not to matter. His dogs failed to sense the scrutiny, the judgment, and he would cling to that, but he knew he was guilty, and that he was being watched.

Disclaimer

These novellas are works of fiction. Given that "fiction" is now understood as the medium in which bullshit is celebrated, but which is still, somehow, subject to fact-checking, and where "escape from reality" is the primary goal—how could it be otherwise, when the memoir owns all rights to reality, and lies are the High Church of Redemptive Nonfiction's dirty little secret?—I want to take a moment to define my fiction. All of the characters, all of the places, all of the events and action and dialogue and description and historical analysis and philosophical maundering is made-up. Even when a character clearly corresponds to a living human being, in the case, for example, of a Chicago mobster or entertainment tycoon, that character is a product of my imagination. I have taken the world as I perceive it and adapted it for the purposes of storytelling. Reality can in no way be preserved. It can only be used—in the service of good or evil, truth or bullshit, compassion or flight from misery (or D: *all of the above*).

About the Author

Photo by Erin Schneider

Born and raised in Minnesota, Gary Amdahl has worked as a janitor, has reviewed books for the *New York Times* and *The Nation,* and most recently was an employee at Dutton's Brentwood Bookstore in Southern California. The author of *Visigoth* (Milkweed Editions, 2006), he is also the recipient of a Jerome Fellowship and a Pushcart Prize. His work has appeared in *Santa Monica Review, Fiction, Gettysburg Review,* and *The Quarterly.* He lives in South California.

Acknowledgments

"I Am Death, or Bartleby the Mobster: a Story of Chicago" was first published in *Santa Monica Review*, Spring 2002. It was written, with the help of Jack Hayes, on whose reporting it is based and without which there would have been no story, in 1992. I would like once again to cry out my deepest gratitude to *SMR*'s editor, Andrew Tonkovich, for putting an end to that terrible decade.

I also want to thank everybody at Milkweed Editions, particularly Emily Cook and Ben Barnhart. They are the most courageous, resourceful, and tireless people in literary publishing. They make the corporate players look like . . . corporate players.

More Fiction from Milkweed Editions

To order books or for more information,
contact Milkweed at (800) 520-6455
or visit our Web site (www.milkweed.org).

The Farther Shore
Matthew Eck

Hell's Bottom, Colorado
Laura Pritchett

The Song of Kahunsha
Anosh Irani

Cracking India
Bapsi Sidhwa

*Pu-239 and Other
Russian Fantasies*
Ken Kalfus

The Crow Eaters
Bapsi Sidhwa

Water
Bapsi Sidhwa

Thirst
Ken Kalfus

Ordinary Wolves
Seth Kantner

Aquaboogie
Susan Straight

Montana 1948
Larry Watson

Roofwalker
Susan Power

Milkweed Editions

Founded in 1979, Milkweed Editions is one of the largest independent, nonprofit literary publishers in the United States. Milkweed publishes with the intention of making a humane impact on society, in the belief that good writing can transform the human heart and spirit. Within this mission, Milkweed publishes in four areas: fiction, nonfiction, poetry, and children's literature for middle-grade readers.

Join Us

Milkweed depends on the generosity of foundations and individuals like you, in addition to the sales of its books. In an increasingly consolidated and bottom-line-driven publishing world, your support allows us to select and publish books on the basis of their literary quality and the depth of their message. Please visit our Web site (www.milkweed.org) or contact us at (800) 520-6455 to learn more about our donor program.

Interior design by Connie Kuhnz. Typeset in Slimbach, created by the prolific and award-winning designer Robert Slimbach for International Typeface Corporation. Printed on acid-free, recycled (100% postconsumer waste) paper by Friesens Corporation.